# Scarred

## Monique Polak

James Lorimer & Company Ltd., Publishers
Toronto

James Lorimer & Company Ltd. acknowledges the support of the Ontario Arts Council. We acknowledge the support of the Government of Canada through the Book Publishing Industry Development Program (BPIDP) for our publishing activities. We acknowledge the support of the Canada Council for the Arts for our publishing program. We acknowledge the support of the Government of Ontario through the Ontario Media Development Corporation's Ontario Book Initiative.

The Canada Council | Le Conseil des Arts
for the Arts | du Canada

ONTARIO ARTS COUNCIL
CONSEIL DES ARTS DE L'ONTARIO

Cover design: Clarke MacDonald

**Library and Archives Canada Cataloguing in Publication**

Polak, Monique
    Scarred /Monique Polak.

(SideStreets)
ISBN 978-1-55028-965-7 (bound).
ISBN 978-1-55028-964-0 (pbk.)

        I. Title. II. Series
PS8631.O43533 2007      jC813'.6      C2007-900352-7

James Lorimer & Company Ltd.,
Publishers
317 Adelaide Street West
Suite 1002
Toronto, Ontario
M5V 1P9
www.lorimer.ca

Distributed in the
U.S. by:
Orca Book Publishers
P.O. Box 468
Custer, WA USA
98240-0468

Printed and bound in Canada

*For Paula*

# Acknowledgements

Special thanks to those of my students who have shared their stories about self-mutilation and their struggle to overcome it. Your openness and courage inspired me to write this book. Thanks to San Diego psychologist Tracy Alderman, author of The Scarred Soul: Understanding and Ending Self-Inflicted Violence, who was kind enough to grant me a phone interview when I first began to research the subject in 2000.

Many thanks to my dad, Maximilien Polak, and to my neighbours Don Kelly and Joanne Morgan for reading the first draft of this manuscript. Thanks to Viva Singer for her friendship and humour. Thanks also to my wonderful editor, Hadley Dyer, and the team at James Lorimer and Company. And, as always, thanks to my daughter Alicia Melamed, and my husband, Michael Shenker. I love you both with all my heart.

# Chapter 1

The mirror was still foggy from my shower, so I rubbed at it with my palm. My reflection grew more clear, as if I was coming out of a fog.

I turned my head to look at the damage. The skin under my right cheekbone looked like a road map, with about a dozen tiny red lines, some running next to each other, others crisscrossing.

I moved closer until all I could see was cheek and a bit of blue eye. The skin looked puffy and inflamed. If it had a voice, it would scream.

It was already hard to believe I'd done this to myself. Dug the tips of my fingernails so deeply into my skin they'd left gashes. One small gash hadn't been enough, hadn't satisfied my desire to hurt myself. No, that would have been like saying I was only going to eat one tortilla chip and then I'd fold up the bag and put it back in the pantry. I'd known all along I wouldn't be able to stop after the first gash.

I'd worked methodically. Once I'd drawn blood, I'd take a deep breath and relax, but only for a few seconds. Then I'd turn my face and move to a fresh spot. Digging, then digging deeper, until the first red drop appeared. Continuing until I'd dug my way across the entire area.

I'd had to bite my lip while I was digging. But the pain hadn't stopped me. No, the sharp, quick silver flashes had just spurred me on. In some weird way, those flashes made me feel alive.

I looked down at the palm of my hand. More little lines, and inside the tips of my fingernails, tiny bits of bloody skin that hadn't come out in the shower.

"Becky! What the hell is taking you so long in there?"

Errol could have used the downstairs bathroom, but as usual, he just wanted to bug me. Bugging me was one of his hobbies. Like making model airplanes and listening to techno music.

I ignored him — my way of bugging him back. He tried the door handle once, then twice, but I'd locked the door.

I heard him sigh in an exaggerated way. "Are you constipated or something?" He started cackling at his own bad joke, but at least now his voice was coming from farther away. He'd probably gone downstairs — or back to his room. Maybe he hadn't even needed the bathroom. Some big brother.

I couldn't stay there forever. But it was hard to stop looking at my cheek. I shut my eyes tight.

Why did I keep doing this to myself?

I took a deep breath. It was time to get a grip. Start taking care of myself. I tugged on the bottom of the mirror — this time, I didn't let myself look at my reflection — instead opening the medicine cabinet behind it.

The Neosporin tube fell out, landing in the sink.

The last person to use it had squeezed from the top, leaving an indentation shaped like a thumbprint. Maybe Dad had nicked himself shaving. Or maybe Errol had cut himself on one of his models.

It couldn't have been Mom. She'd have squeezed from the bottom and made sure to put the Neosporin back in its proper place next to the Band-Aids.

I folded the tube so it made a neat, flat edge like the corner of an envelope. A blob of white cream torpedoed out of the tube and landed — *splat* — on the mirror, the way it happens with toothpaste when you squeeze too hard. Then I leaned into the mirror and wiped up the antibiotic cream. It left a greasy white smudge, but I got most of it.

Gently, careful to use the padded part of my fingertip, I applied the Neosporin to the tiny red roads. I didn't rub. I dabbed, barely touching the skin. The white cream disappeared, absorbed by the gashes.

Hopefully, it would help them heal.

*Poor you*, I thought. What I meant was *poor me* — only sometimes it was easier to pretend that some of the stuff going on in my life was happening to someone else.

*You really have to start taking better care of yourself, Becky Sanger.*

*Poor you.*

I mean, *poor me.*

Still wet from the shower, my dark hair looked straight. Once it dried, it would frizz up like the top of a Q-tip. My eyes looked tired. At least the blood on my cheek had begun to coagulate. But the Neosporin added a sickly shine.

If only I could stay in here till my skin healed. Of course, that didn't make any sense. It would take days before the gashes turned pink and even longer before my skin knit itself together and the gashes disappeared, leaving nothing but a few tiny scars.

I knew because I'd done this before.

Band-Aids wouldn't be a good idea. My skin needed to breathe. Air would help the tiny gashes heal. Rest was good, too.

At least now I felt calm enough to sleep. Before, I'd been so keyed up, I could hardly keep track of my thoughts.

I looked into the mirror again. This time, I made myself concentrate on other things beside the gashes. Tight curls were already springing up around my face. I didn't bother patting them down. There was no point fighting fate. I had Dad's unmanageable hair. It was just my luck Errol had been the one to get Mom's straight, glossy hair and long, dark eyelashes. All wasted on him.

Before I left the bathroom, I stood inside a little longer, listening at the door for sounds. I could hear the soft hum of Mom and Dad's voices in the kitchen. I imagined them discussing Mom's latest real estate deal — or what wine they were having with dinner.

I hoped Errol was downstairs, too. I wasn't in the mood for his wisecracks.

I pulled my bathrobe tighter around my waist. A birthday present from my parents, it was made of pale blue chenille, with tiny white-and-silver skates all over it, as if they were dancing.

"Made for you — our darling skater," Mom said when they gave it to me. I'd had the feeling she'd wanted to say more, but because it was my birthday, she held it in. Something about how I'd given up competitive skating. Or what a shame it was she'd had to buy me a size large, since the mediums came in nicer colours.

The blades on the skates were embroidered with metallic thread. They'd seemed to glisten, just like they did now in the bathroom's white light.

I shivered as I imagined the blades carving the cool, smooth surface of the ice like sharp finger-nails on flesh.

I didn't realize how tired I was until I turned

over the top sheet of my bed and crawled in. I'd been on the ice, teaching, for four hours straight. *You deserve a good night's sleep*, I told myself. *You've been working hard — doing a good job, too. Some of those little girls are really getting the hang of it. They're finding their skating feet. And that Amy, she's something else. Quiet as a mouse, but talented. Really talented.*

I lay in bed, staring at the ceiling and trying not to move a muscle on my face. If I did, the pain would set in.

I heard Mom's footsteps coming up the stairs. She stopped outside my room.

"Gone to sleep already, Becks?" she whispered from the hallway.

"Uh-huh." I tried to make my voice sound even sleepier than I was.

She didn't move from her spot in the hallway.

"Listen, I'm sorry about before. I shouldn't have said anything about your weight. I know I'm too critical, but —" she stopped for a second as if she was searching for the right words, "I only want the best for you, Becky. Really I do."

"I know, Mom."

"Can I come in and chat?" Then, without warning, she opened my door and switched on the lights. I hate when she does stuff like that.

I lifted my hands to my face.

"Turn it off!" I said, raising my voice and breathing from the top of my chest. "The light's hurting my eyes!"

She flipped the switch back off. But I could still see her shadow in the doorway.

I felt my breathing go back to normal. "I'm too tired to talk."

"I'll just kiss you good-night."

The way she said it made me feel like she wanted something. Something more than a kiss. Maybe she wanted me to tell her she was a good mom. But I couldn't.

I winced as she stepped towards my bed. Then I lifted my head from the pillow and presented my cheek for a kiss. The left cheek.

I willed her not to try to kiss my other cheek, too.

At least I was safe in the dark. Tomorrow, I'd put on a thick layer of foundation makeup to cover the gashes. I'd smile at the breakfast table and make conversation with my parents. I'd let Errol tease me, and later, I'd be a first-rate skating teacher.

No one would know that tonight, after dinner, I'd dug my fingernails into my right cheek for so long and so deeply I'd made that map of gashes.

At least, this time, I hadn't used the Swiss Army knife.

# Chapter 2

"Can you show us a spin, Miss Becky? Ple-ee-ease!"

"Later." When Tara pouted, I added, "I promise."

Tara's face was round as a penny. The most talkative girl in my group, she was always asking questions or making comments.

Amy was already on the other side of the rink, practising her forward stroking. Amy talked less, but you could tell she was intense. I thought about making her come back to the sideboards, where I was working with the other girls. But when I saw the determined way she was skating, one foot crossing over the other in perfect rhythm, I left her alone.

I knew exactly how she was feeling, because when I was her age, I'd felt that way, too. She was completely focused on her stroking, enjoying the sound her skates made as they carved the surface of the ice. Oblivious to everything else. Safe.

Most of my girls were beginners. But when Amy's mom dropped her off on the first day of sports camp, she'd made sure to tell me how Amy had been skating since she was three.

"She's a tremendously gifted athlete," Mrs. Gross had said, flipping her frosted blonde hair away from her forehead, and looking me in the eye as if she wanted to be sure I knew how lucky I was to be working with her gifted daughter.

I knew her type — Mrs. Gross was a queen bee skating mom. This was my second summer working at Côte St. Luc Sports Camp and I'd met other queen bees before. It was all about Mrs. Gross. If Amy was gifted, she wanted the credit. My mom had been a queen bee, too. That is, until I'd gone and disappointed her.

"I'm really looking forward to working with Amy. And if she's as strong as you say, I'll make sure she does an accelerated program," I'd said, figuring that would satisfy Mrs. Gross. "You know, I started when I was three, too."

"How old are you now?" Mrs. Gross had asked.

"Fifteen. And a half."

I could feel Mrs. Gross assessing me. When her eyes landed on my hips, I knew she was thinking I was heavy for a figure skater. Figure skaters have muscular legs and small breasts. My body didn't exactly qualify. Mrs. Gross was thinking maybe that was why I hadn't made it in the competitive skating world. It would also explain

13

why I spent my summers teaching basic figure skating to first-graders.

Tara was holding onto the boards with one hand. You could tell her crash helmet was a hand-me-down because of all the scratches. Her red chiffon skirt was loose at the waist, hanging lower on one side than the other.

"You need to let go," I told her. I reached for her hand, but she refused to loosen her grip on the boards.

Tara bit her lower lip. "What if I fall?"

"Ah-ha!" I said, clapping my hands together to get all the girls' attention. "Time for a really important lesson," I called out. "You ladies are about to learn lesson number one: How to fall."

I skated backwards until I was a few metres from the boards. I could feel the whole class watching me. Even Amy had stopped stroking and rejoined the rest of the group.

I took a few pushes and then, because I wanted to keep my promise to Tara, I did a spin. I kept my head and spine straight and still, then I extended my arms and raised my right leg. When I brought my leg in, and my arms back to my body so they were crossed over my chest, I started picking up speed. I spun faster and faster, until everything around me — the girls in my group, the ice, the scoreboard and the stands — turned to white fuzz.

"Wow!" I heard Tara call out, but by then, I was already tumbling to the ice.

I threw my hands forward and bent my knees as if I was about to sit down on a chair. Then I fell forward, landing noiselessly on the ice. A perfect fall — if I do say so myself. The sharp teeth at the ends of my skate blades glistened as they caught the light.

"Miss Becky! Are you okay?" Randy, a freckle-faced girl who wore her red hair in tight braids, asked. But when she realized the others were laughing, Randy started laughing, too. How come kids love it so much when their skating teacher takes a spill?

I shook the frost from my gloves. "Lesson two: If you're going to be a figure skater," I called out, without getting up from the ice, "you can't be afraid to fall. So we're going to spend a little time this morning practising our falls."

There was some rustling in the group as they made room for Amy, who was the first to break away and skate out to where I was standing. Not only was she my best skater, she was a head taller than the other girls. A couple of seconds later, Amy was gliding on her knees; then she flipped onto her back, kicking her feet up in the air and bicycling them. If things didn't work out for her as a skater, she could always try acting. I had a feeling her mom would like that, too.

Amy turned to look at me.

"That was very dramatic," I told her.

We got up from the ice and skated back to the rest of the class. I could tell from the way a couple of girls were clutching the boards that they still weren't keen to work on their falls.

"Look," I told them, "there's really nothing to it. Just remember to keep your hands in front of you. That way they'll catch you when you fall."

"Hey!" I said when I noticed Randy taking off her gloves and shoving them into the kangaroo pocket of her sweatshirt. "Gloves on!" I raised my voice so the girls would know I meant business.

"Never, ever take your gloves off on the ice! You wouldn't want a skate blade running over your bare hand."

My voice trailed off as I thought about my Swiss Army knife, safely stashed in the pencil tin on top of my desk. I thought about how, when I opened it up and released the blade, there'd be tiny dry rusty spots on it — my own blood.

Without meaning to, I ran my fingers against my right cheek. I'd done a good job covering the gashes with foundation, but now the skin stung when I touched it. I knew from experience that in another day or two the skin would be less sensitive to touch.

A small voice brought me back to the rink. "Hey, Miss Becky! Are you listening? You showed us falling, but is there a trick for getting up, too?" Tara, who was still standing at the boards, wanted to know.

"Hey, you're way ahead of the class."

Tara grinned. This time, when I reached for her

hand, she gave it to me. "Come show us a fall. Getting up is lesson three."

*\*\**

"There's just one rule you need to learn about getting up," I told the girls once they were all down on the ice. "You can't rely on someone else to do it for you. Okay then, ladies, up you go!"

Amy and Randy were making snow angels, brushing their arms and legs against the ice.

"Hey, quit that!" I told them, raising my voice. This was another lesson all the girls needed to hear. "Lying on the ice like that is really dangerous —"

"You wouldn't want to get runned over by a skate blade," Amy said, cutting me off. Because she was usually so quiet, the sound of her voice — hard and surprisingly grown-up — surprised me. It took me a second to realize she was imitating me. Little brat.

"Quite right," I told her. "Only it's 'run over,' not 'runned over.'"

Randy raised herself up from her knees. "My daddy used a chair to teach me getting up," she said.

"That's how a lot of people teach getting up," I told the girls. "But when you get up on your own — without someone's help, or without a chair — you learn something else that's super important for figure skaters. Come to think of it, it's lesson number four. Can any of you guess what it is?"

"Balance!" Amy called out, watching my face. I had a feeling she was trying to get back on my good side. This was the most she'd talked so far this session.

"Amy's right. Skating is about not being afraid to take a tumble, picking yourself up when you do, not lying around on the ice — and balance."

\*\*\*

"Getting your balance is hard," I heard Randy tell Tara later, when they were lining up to get off the ice. I was standing by the boards, making sure none of them bumped into each other.

"I don't know if I'll ever get my balance," Tara said, shrugging her shoulders as she walked out into the stands.

"You will. Miss Becky will help you. She's a really good teacher."

When I smiled, my right cheek hurt.

Randy dropped her voice. "She's pretty, too," she added.

This time, I tried not to smile.

"Really pretty," Tara said. When she turned around, I knew she was checking to see if I was listening. So I leaned down and pretended to inspect a patch of dark ice.

"But how come she wears so much makeup to skating lessons?"

# Chapter 3

Every counsellor had lunch duty three times a week. That meant we ate with our kids, usually out on the picnic tables behind the Côte St. Luc recreation centre. Côte St. Luc is only a fifteen or twenty-minute drive from downtown Montreal. But if you were out on the field behind the rec centre, with the birds chirping in the spruce trees and the air smelling of freshly mown grass, it was easy to forget you were so close to the centre of the city.

The streets in Côte St. Luc are not very interesting. Most went in straight lines and a lot of the houses looked the same: brick bungalows, many of them attached in pairs. But the sprawling green parks, like the one behind the rec centre, helped make the neighbourhood special.

It was Tuesday, so I was on my own for lunch. The other instructors liked having a break from their campers. Not me. When I'm with my girls, I'm totally focused on them. Time passes really quickly and sometimes it's hard to believe I get paid for what I do. I like how kids say whatever's on their mind — unlike adults, who have a way of saying one thing, when they really mean something else.

I ordered a club sandwich from the canteen — no fries, just coleslaw on the side. Mom would be glad I'd resisted the fries, but she wouldn't approve of the coleslaw. "Full of mayonnaise," she'd say, turning up her nose.

I could've sat with two other counsellors who'd ordered their food at the same time as me. I recognized one, a soccer specialist named Beth, from last year. She lived a few blocks over from my house and we'd walked to camp together a few times. The girl with Beth must have been new, but judging from the dirty smudge on one elbow of her striped jersey, I figured she worked in soccer, too.

I sawed at my sandwich with the white plastic knife the woman at the canteen had handed me. Slivers of turkey fell out onto the plate, and still I didn't manage to cut through the toasted bread. *Useless knife*, I thought, as I lifted the sandwich to my mouth and took a bite.

I was supposed to slow down when I ate, chew twenty times before every bite and really taste the food. Mom had read that in *Shape* magazine and she'd come rushing up to my room to share the tip as if she thought it was life-changing. Some moms are into self-improvement; mine's into daughter-improvement.

Mom had pretty much given up on Errol since he'd dropped out of college. She'd tried harassing him and then bribing him into going back to school, but neither of those strategies had worked. So now, she'd turned her focus to me.

I knew it really bugged her that I'd been putting on weight. I'd started getting heavier around the time I gave up competitive skating — and instead of losing the weight, I'd only put on more.

Being out on the ice builds an appetite. So does handling a group of seven-year-olds, I thought, as I remembered the way Amy had imitated me and what I'd overheard Tara say about my makeup.

After I'd finished the sandwich, I wiped my mouth with a paper napkin. I was careful to keep its rough surface away from my right cheek.

I didn't mean to listen in on Beth's conversation with her new friend, but they were talking really loud, so it was hard not to.

"Thank God payday's on Friday," Beth was saying. "I'm saving up for a new iPod. I've been losing my mind since the old one konked out."

I reached into my gym bag for my sketchbook. At first, all I did was play with the spiral binding, pulling at the wire on one end and rolling it between my fingers, testing its sharpness. Not very sharp, I decided. Definitely not sharp enough to break skin.

*Don't go there*, I told myself. *Get a grip. You*

*were about to open the sketchbook. Go ahead. Open it. And stop thinking about weird stuff like breaking skin.*

I flipped the sketchbook open to the last page I'd worked on. There, in one corner, was a tiny sketch — no bigger than a stamp — of a single skate, its lace untied and curling round at its ends like a snake.

On the page before that I'd tried to sketch some of the girls in my group from memory. I hadn't done a very good job. Tara's face wasn't round enough, and Randy's red braids looked like sausages with bows on them.

I'd also tried to do a line drawing of Amy's mom. I'd put one of those sound bubbles over her head. In it, I'd written, "Have I told you how talented my daughter is?"

Poor Amy. Only after this morning's class, I didn't feel quite so sorry for her. The kid had a bad attitude.

Then I remembered the determined way she'd been stroking around the rink and I turned to a fresh page and tried to draw that. I started with a side view of her head, her straight nose and long chin. I added an eye and eyelashes, trying to capture the way Amy focused on the ice in front of her. I didn't worry too much about details. I just wanted to get the idea down on the page.

Then, without planning to, I moved to the other side of the page and started drawing a line. It curved into an oval, then it went round and round, the way Amy had gone around the rink at the beginning of class. For a second, I felt as if I was skating with my pen. *Yes*, I thought, Amy was a show-off, but there was no doubt that girl could skate. Really skate.

The wooden bench where I'd gone to sit was just down the hall from the boys' locker room. A couple of boy campers had gone in and out while I'd been eating my sandwich, probably to get their sandwiches and juice boxes from their lockers. They were so different from the girls I worked with, jostling each other and making burping noises.

Just then, an older boy came lumbering out of the locker room. He was still wearing knee pads and a face mask.

"I tell them to keep their eyes on the puck," he muttered to himself, "but they don't get it. They just don't get it."

"It's only the second week of camp," I said as I retraced the oval lines, this time in the opposite direction. I hadn't meant to say anything. The words had just popped out. I scribbled harder, trying to pretend it wasn't me who'd said them.

But the boy in the face mask wasn't fooled.

"I know it's only the second week, but it's still kind of depressing, don't you think?"

He was standing behind me, and when I realized he could look into my sketchbook, I closed it. This was all my fault, of course. I'd wanted to be alone, but then I'd gone and started up a conversation.

23

The bench rocked as the boy sat down next to me. At first, I tried ignoring him, thinking that might make him go away. When that didn't work, I figured I didn't have any choice, so I turned to look at him. Might as well get this over with.

When he lifted his face mask, I noticed his pale blue eyes — not much darker than the colour of ice. Where had I seen eyes that colour before?

"Becky?"

I gulped. It was Tory Featherstone. We'd taken skating lessons together at the rec centre when we were really little. And later, he'd played competitive hockey at the same arena where I'd trained. I hadn't seen him since I'd stopped competing and he and his family had moved away from Côte St. Luc.

"Geez, Becky, it's been forever."

"How are you doing, Tory?" It was a pretty weird coincidence, bumping into him like this.

"I'm fine. Except for the fact I can't seem to teach my kids to keep their eyes on the darned puck. How 'bout you, Becky? Still competing?"

"Nah, I gave it up."

Tory raised his eyebrows.

"You're kidding," he said. "You really had what it takes."

"I lost it."

When Tory frowned, his eyebrows met. "Hey, Becky, it's good to see you. How 'bout we go for a coffee after camp today? We could shoot the breeze, catch up, you know …"

I took a deep breath and dropped my eyes to the cover of my sketchbook. There was a stylized image of a woman on it, stretching her torso forward like a cat.

Running into Tory here — at the rink where we'd both learned to skate — was bringing back all sorts of memories. I saw myself in my pink chiffon skating skirt, spinning on the ice, Tory zooming by with his friends. I blinked to make the picture go away. I didn't like thinking about my skating days.

"Sorry, Tory. I can't."

"What do you mean you can't?"

I opened my sketchbook to a fresh page. "I just can't," I said as I began to draw a triangle. I added lines to give it depth, then a few small rectangular bits coming out from the sides. Slowly, it started looking like a club sandwich.

When Tory got up from the bench, I didn't lift my head from the sketchbook.

# Chapter 4

On Tuesdays, the house was always quiet after camp. That's because every Tuesday, from five to six p.m., Errol and my parents have a regular appointment with Dr. Sewell, the shrink. If you ask me, old Sewell isn't doing Errol much good. All Errol does is build model airplanes and listen to techno music.

Part of me likes coming home to an empty house — perfectly quiet except for the hum of the air conditioner and the noise I made when I kicked off my sneakers at the front door. I didn't have to tell anyone about my day and endure Mom's opinions on topics like the importance of eating raw veggies and their effect on the digestive tract. Mom had a way of getting a little too into the details.

On the other hand, sometimes when I'm alone, I get into trouble.

I could've gone to the den and turned on the TV, caught the end of some talk show, or I could've laid down on the couch in the living room and flipped through one of Mom's wellness magazines, but instead I headed upstairs. With every step, I thought about how I was getting closer to my room, to my desk … and to my pencil tin.

I could still turn around and go downstairs. Watch TV, read, take out my sketchbook, or grab something to eat. A piece of chocolate or maple fudge would be nice. Not that Mom kept stuff like that in the house. Her idea of an afternoon snack was carrots and celery sticks. Rabbit food. I could imagine Mom standing in the kitchen, waving a peeled carrot at me. "Think how good you'll feel after you've loaded up on beta carotene," she'd say.

But it was already too late to turn back. The door to my room was shut — just like I'd left it. When I opened it, the first thing I noticed was the fresh scent of the cucumber melon body lotion I'd put on before camp. But I could also tell Mom had been inside my room. The bedspread had been pulled tight so there were no wrinkles and when I turned it down, I knew the sheets would have perfect hospital corners.

I groaned. Why did she have to be so nosy? You'd think with all the trouble she and Dad were having with Errol, she'd spend a little time rethinking her idea of motherhood. But no, not her. She was too busy improving other people.

My eyes shifted to my desk. The pencil tin was in its usual place in the top left corner, lined up behind my blotter, undisturbed. Phew.

I could've gone over and taken out the Swiss Army knife right then, but I didn't. It was like I was playing a game with myself — seeing how long I could resist. I got a certain pleasure just knowing the knife was there, safely stashed at the bottom of my pencil tin.

I lay down on the bed. I rolled over so I was looking at the wall, not my desk. I could still see the Scotch Tape marks from where I'd taken down the poster of Oksana Baiul, the Ukrainian figure skater who'd won a gold medal at the 1994 Winter Olympics in Lillehammer, Norway.

In 1994, I was four years old — already on my second pair of skates.

A fat black ant crawled along the inside of the window frame next to where the poster had been. I propped myself up and cracked open the window, then I took a deep breath and blew the ant out onto the balcony. *There you go little guy*, I thought as I watched him totter along the wood. *You're better off outside. If Errol had found you, he'd have crushed you to death and flushed you down the toilet.* Errol hates bugs.

I settled my head back on my pillow. But I still didn't let myself turn so I'd be facing my desk. This time, I tried looked up at the ceiling. The rest of the room was pale blue, but the ceiling was a crisp clean white. The colour of clouds.

A touch greyer and it would be the colour of ice.

"Who's that boy you were talking to?" Tara had wanted to know. Leave it to her to ask another embarrassing question. She'd spotted Tory and me during lunch when she'd come back inside the rec centre to use the bathroom. Then she'd lowered her voice, "He's cute."

"Oh him," I'd said. "He's an old friend."

Suddenly, I remembered the nickname Tory and the other boys at the rink had had for me: Ice Princess. They'd say it when I passed them outside the arena, or when I walked by them in the stands. At the time, I'd liked the nickname. It had made me feel special — like I really was an ice princess. I remembered walking a little taller when they'd say it, straightening my back and shoulders as if I was wearing a jeweled crown on my head.

*Ice Princess*. At first, I'd smiled as I said the words out loud. But now, they began to take on a different meaning — one I'd never thought about before and that was not at all flattering. Had the boys been calling me icy? Cold? I was never very good at dealing with my feelings. That was why I hadn't agreed to meet up with Tory after camp. Seeing him had stirred up too many old feelings and memories — feelings and memories that confused and frightened me.

It occurred to me now that even when Tory and his friends were in first and second grade, they had already known about my coldness.

I was no princess, but they'd been right all along. I was cold. Icy, even. It was one more way I wasn't any good. One more defect. Add it to the list — along with my weight and my lack of self-discipline.

Slowly, I raised myself up from my bed and walked over to my desk. I'd made this same walk so many times before, feeling more or less the same way, like I was on autopilot. I knew the walk took fourteen steps. *Thirteen ... fourteen.*

I took the pencil tin from the desk. I pushed two pens and a marker over to the side of the tin so I could reach to the bottom. *Ahh*, I thought as my fingers ran across the plastic casing of my Swiss Army knife. There was something comforting about its familiar smoothness.

In a weird way, the knife was like an old friend. The kind who knows everything about you.

I'd found it at the bus stop near our house the winter I'd stopped competing. At first, I kept it in the pencil tin. Later, when my thoughts started spinning too fast, I started using it.

I'll never forget the first time. Mom and Dad were giving Errol a hard time for failing some pop quiz. Errol stormed into his room, slamming his door so hard my walls shook. Mom came running upstairs after him. I should have waited till the whole thing blew over, but I guess some part of me thought I could help.

I opened my door just when Mom reached the landing. Our eyes met and she looked at me as if she'd never seen me before. She just shook her head without saying a word. But I could tell exactly what she was thinking. That I was getting fatter and fatter. That I was turning out to be just as big a disappointment as Errol.

I'd closed my door and taken out the Swiss Army knife. At first, all I did was rub the casing against the inside of my left wrist. But that hadn't been enough. I released the blade, running it against the skin, but without exerting any pressure. That hadn't satisfied me either.

The first cut, the first drop of blood brought a kind of relief I'd never felt before. I'd even been able to tune out the sounds of Mom and Errol shouting, and of Dad trudging up the stairs, pleading with them both to cut it out.

That's when the Swiss Army knife became my friend. The thought sent a chill through my spine. *My friend?* The knife wasn't my friend. What kind of friend would hurt you? Make you bleed? No, the knife was my enemy. I knew better than anyone else what harm it could do.

But now, even knowing what I did, I still couldn't resist. It was as if it had some strange hold on me.

I brought the knife back to my bed. I told myself I'd just play with it — rub it between my fingers, caress its shiny red casing, trace the raised surface where the white cross was. Maybe I'd flick the knife open, examine the blade, the dried specks of blood.

But who was I fooling? There was no way I could just look at it.

My fingers trembled as I flicked it open. The blade was only about an inch long, but I knew how sharp it was. Easily sharp enough to break skin.

I turned my left arm so the pale skin on the inside of my wrist was exposed. A row of faint, slightly raised white lines crisscrossed my veins — scars from where I'd cut myself before. I felt my heart race as I used the knife to slice the skin.

*One, two, three, four, five,* and it was done. Five quick slices. Deep enough to break the skin. Deep enough to draw blood. *Ahh,* I thought, as I felt every muscle in my body begin to relax.

It was only when I watched the blood trickle down the side of my arm and onto the floor that I noticed the pain, a deep ache that seemed to shoot from my wrist right up to my shoulder, then back down to my chest.

I raised my hand to my mouth to muffle the sound of my moaning. But then I remembered no one was home. I didn't have to worry about anyone hearing me — and discovering my secret.

"Oww," I whimpered, but then the whimper grew stronger and louder, and turned into a wail. *"Oww!!"*

*See,* I told myself as I felt the first few hot tears stream down my cheeks. *You're no ice queen. You can feel pain.*

# Chapter 5

The steel blade glistened as it caught the light from the halogen bulbs in the ceiling. Thick orange-red droplets hung from the side of the blade, like the buds of an exotic flower.

Dad didn't lift his eyes from the butcher-block counter, where he was cutting a slab of pizza into small rectangles. "Red pizza for dinner! Pizza rosa!" he announced in a terrible imitation of an Italian accent. I laughed. Dad was always funniest when he wasn't trying to be funny.

"We picked it up at the Italian bakery on Upper Lachine Road on the way home. I mean on the way back to our casa."

"You're so clever," Mom told him.

"You have such fine taste in husbands."

The two of them were like each other's fan club.

"I've got a lovely green salad to go with the pizza. I really want to eat more salads this summer. It's part of my plan to shed a few pounds," Mom said, smiling, then lifting her eyes in my direction.

I groaned to myself. Mom had a great body, even for a woman her age. There was no way she needed to lose weight.

"You look terrific, Gwennie. Always have and always will," Dad said as he transferred the pizza slices to a platter.

I couldn't see Mom's face, but I knew she'd be smiling. Mom ate up compliments. It was a good thing they didn't have any calories.

The fridge was open, and from where I was standing, all I could see of Mom were her feet. She was wearing new bronze sandals, and when she reached into the fridge for the salad, the beaded tassels on her shoes jingled. Her bright red toenails looked like they'd been freshly polished.

She put the salad bowl on the counter, then turned to face me.

"I bought low-cal oil-and-vinegar dressing." From the way she smiled, you'd think she'd gone and got me some amazing present.

"Great," I said, trying to sound excited. "Anything I can do to help?"

Dad wiped his hands on a dishtowel. "You're a good kid. You know that, don't you, Becky? Always offering to help out. Your mom and I really appreciate your attitude. Don't we, Gwennie?"

"We certainly do," Mom said. "Put this out on the table, please. Near where you're sitting." She handed me the bottle of dressing without looking at me. No matter what she said, I knew Mom was disappointed in me. She'd never forgiven me for giving up competitive skating and putting on weight. I'd ruined Mom's dream of having a daughter who was a world-class athlete and who didn't have an extra ounce of fat on her body.

"You can tell your brother it's time for dinner," Dad said, tossing the dishtowel over the metal bar on the oven door. When the towel fell to the ground, Mom made a *tsk*-ing sound and reached down to pick it up. Then she folded it into three equal sections and hung it over the bar, so the towel was perfectly centered.

When my dad rolled his eyes at me, I cracked a small smile. Quickly, before Mom caught us. She didn't have such a great sense of humour when it came to jokes about herself.

I left the kitchen and walked to the foot of the stairs. I cupped my hands over my mouth.

"Errol!" I shouted, so he'd hear me over the dull throb of his techno music. "Pizza's on!"

"Couldn't you have gone upstairs to get him, Becky?" I could hear Dad drop the serrated knife into the sink. Was it just me or were there knives everywhere?

"Hey, I thought you were just saying how I was the perfect daughter," I called back to Dad.

I heard Mom turn on the tap. "He never said that," she muttered.

When Errol came down to the dining room, he

pulled out his chair without saying a word to any of us. I figured that meant Dr. Sewell hadn't made any major breakthroughs that afternoon.

"Well, it's certainly nice to be eating together as a family." Mom's voice sounded cheerful, but her jaw was tight. You could tell that hanging out with her kids was a bit of a strain.

"Very nice," Dad agreed as he bit into his pizza.

"Edward," my mom said, tapping the skin between her lips and her nose. There was a glob of tomato sauce smack in the middle of Dad's moustache.

"Oops!" he said, wiping it clean, then turning to Mom for her approval.

Mom nodded.

I reached over for a second piece of pizza. I scanned the serving plate, looking for the biggest rectangle. It was over in the far corner. Mom wouldn't say anything if I had two pieces, but I knew I'd hear about it if I went for a third.

The tomato sauce had a nice tangy flavour. They made it at the Italian bakery. For a few seconds, I concentrated on the taste. When there was only a little corner left, I started wishing I'd eaten more slowly. Chewed twenty times before each bite, the way I was supposed to. If Mom got up from the table, I might be able to grab another piece. Dad and Errol wouldn't be keeping count the way Mom did.

Two pieces of pizza seemed to be enough for Errol. He was drumming his fingers on the edge of the table, as if the techno music was still playing in his head.

Mom and Dad exchanged a look. They didn't say a word, but I could tell they were communicating. From the corner of her eye, Mom looked at Errol's fingers, then back at my dad, and raised her eyebrows. Dad shook his head no and smiled. He didn't stand up to Mom very often. But he didn't want her to tell Errol to quit tapping.

Mom nodded back at Dad. She reached for her knife and cut what was left of her piece of pizza — she'd only taken one piece — into even smaller pieces. Then she turned to me. If she couldn't criticize Errol, she must have figured I was fair game.

"Why are you wearing long sleeves again?" she asked. "It's July, for goodness sake. And you still haven't worn that cute pink T-shirt we picked up for you when we were in Toronto."

The navy blue T-shirt I was wearing had sleeves so low they covered not just my wrists, but even part of my palms. Suddenly, I became aware of my wrists and how sore they were. Once the bleeding had stopped, I'd put on Neosporin and a layer of Band-Aids.

But now I made a point of not looking down at my T-shirt — or at where the sleeves lapped over my hands. I didn't want to draw attention to myself. Besides, I didn't have much time. When Mom was on the attack, you had to mount a counter-offensive — quickly. If you didn't, she'll just keep firing.

"It's freezing in here," I said. "I don't know why you guys always the keep air-conditioning on so low."

"Your mother likes it when the house is cool. Especially these days."

"You mean because she's having hot flashes?" It was the first thing Errol had said since he'd sat down. He was smiling now, entertained, I guess, by his own stupid joke.

Dad glanced over at Mom to check her feelings weren't hurt, then he looked at Errol. "That's no way to speak to your mother."

At least now the pressure was off me.

"You're right, Errol. That's why I like to keep the air-conditioning on low," Mom said. "Menopause, by the way, is a perfectly normal biological function. I might be getting older, but I do my best to take care of myself."

Then she looked across the table at me. "I'd still like to see you in that pink T-shirt." I felt her studying the T-shirt I was wearing and tried not to feel self-conscious. "Besides, pink suits you."

Errol kicked me under the table.

"Hey sis," he said. "Today in therapy, we were talking about how Mom's hit menopause. And how it's making her even crankier than usual."

"Errol!" Dad said sharply.

"I don't think Mom's cranky," I said. "She's just a perfectionist. She expects a lot from us."

Mom smiled. For the first time since dinner started, her jaw looked more relaxed. She obviously thought that being a perfectionist and expecting a lot from people were good things.

"Did they tell you what else Dr. Sewell said?" Errol's smile got even wider. He looked as pleased with himself as if he'd trapped an earwig and was about to torture it to death. "You're going to love this: Dr. Sewell wants you to come to therapy, too."

I looked up at my parents. I could feel my eyes flashing.

"What's he talking about?" I asked. "There's nothing wrong with me."

And for a moment there, sitting at the dining room table with the rest of my crazy family, I believed it.

# Chapter 6

Tara rubbed the back of her shins. "This is too hard. I can't do it. I can't," she whimpered.

We'd spent the first half of class reviewing falling down and getting back up, and now we were doing some more work on balance. I'd asked the girls to get into single file and march behind me, lifting one foot at a time as they followed me across the ice. I'd even brought the CD of "Swan Lake", so I could play the marching part over the loudspeaker: *Ta-ta-ta-tum. Ta-ta-ta-tum.* But Tara kept toppling over and having to pick herself up. Her blonde curls were covered in frost.

"I can't," she said, looking up at me from the ice. If she hadn't had that round, angelic face, she might have got on my nerves.

I helped her up. "You know it's dangerous to say you *can't* do something." Her arm was little and thin and I was careful not to tug too hard.

"Dangerous? You mean like not wearing a seat belt?"

"Yeah, something like that," I said. Then I clapped my hands to get the rest of the class's attention.

They weren't in quite as neat a line as I'd have liked. Tara wasn't the only one having trouble. Two of the girls at the back were holding on to each other's elbows. I sighed. They'd never find their balance that way.

I raised my voice so all the girls could hear me over Tchaikovsky's march. "I was just telling Tara how it's dangerous — almost as dangerous as not wearing a seat belt — when we say we can't do something. Because you know what? If we say we *can't* do something, there's only one thing that's going to happen: we *won't* be able to do it. So, as of right now, the words 'I can't' are strictly forbidden in our skating class. All any of us are allowed to say is, 'I'm having trouble with getting up from the ice or finding my balance.' No more 'I can'ts!'"

I scanned my skaters' faces to see if they'd gotten my point. I wanted them to understand that a positive attitude has a lot to do with skating. Amy was the only one who nodded. The others were still busy trying to find — and keep — their balance.

"Oh no!" Tara said when she took another tumble on the ice. At least this time, she hadn't said, "I can't." Even if she hadn't yet quite found her

41

balance, maybe I had managed to teach her something after all.

Now was probably a good time for the soccer ball. When I'd seen Beth outside the locker room that morning, I'd asked if she had a spare soccer ball I could borrow. I'd discovered the summer before that having the girls roll a ball on the ice and bending down to catch it was another good way to help them with their balance. So I skated over to the front of the stands, where I'd left the ball under one of the seats.

I like having surprises for my skaters. And props. It helps keeps class lively.

But as it turned out, I was the one who got a surprise.

"Hey," a voice called as I climbed off the ice and swung open the wooden door that led to the stands. It was coming from somewhere up high. I craned my neck to see who it was.

Tory. He was wearing his hockey gear and his legs were stretched out on the bench in front of him. His eyes were an even paler blue than I remembered. He had an apple core in one hand. I could tell he'd been watching me and the thought made me a little uncomfortable.

"I'm on my apple break," he said, waving the apple core in the air in front of him.

I reached down for the soccer ball and held it to my chest.

"I like how you work with your skaters," Tory said. "And I like how you told them never to say they can't. That's a really good point. If you say you can't do something, you'll never be able to do it."

I felt him watching my face, checking for my reaction. I lifted the soccer ball higher, so it covered my right cheek.

What exactly was Tory getting at? And then, all at once, I got it. He was talking about me. How I'd told him I couldn't go for coffee after camp. "I can't," I'd said. "I just can't."

"You always were a smart aleck," I said, as I started to turn away from him. "I'd better get back to my girls. We're working on balance. A couple of them still aren't getting it, so I figured I'd try working with the soccer ball next." I hadn't meant to say so much.

"You were always an ice queen." Tory said the words under his breath, but I heard them. He'd wanted me to hear them.

I was just about to turn back and say something — to ask him what he'd meant by that — when he muttered something else. "It's one of the things I always liked about you."

I dropped my head. I didn't want Tory to know he'd made me blush.

*One* of the things he *liked* about me? Did that mean there were more?

I leaned into the ice as I skated briskly back to my girls. I made a point of not looking back at the stands. I only turned around once I was facing my group. I scanned the stands. Tory was gone.

I should have been glad. I hadn't liked him spying on me, or making personal comments. Instead, I was disappointed.

But there wasn't time for that. I had to focus on my skaters, help them get their balance. Once they had the hang of it, we could go on to the harder moves.

I rolled the ball along the ice, not too fast, aiming it so it would land just in front of Tara.

She laughed when she reached down for it. For a moment, she seemed to forget the trouble she'd been having all morning.

"Okay, Tara," I called out, "now go ahead and roll the ball over to someone else. It's a game. So let's have some fun here!"

When Tara laughed, her face got even rounder. She rolled the ball over to Randy, who caught hold of it and passed it to Amy. Only instead of passing on the ball like she was supposed to, Amy took it in her arms and started skating with it, heading all the way to the other side of the rink.

"Hey, Amy! Come back here!" Randy called out.

"Amy!" I called out, too. I tried to make my voice sound serious, angry even. But I couldn't really blame Amy. She'd found her balance long ago and now she was bored. I'd have felt the same way, if I were her.

I had to start thinking about designing an individualized program for her. Something told me her mother would approve of the idea.

Someone was tugging on my leggings. It was Tara, and when she let go, I saw she was perfectly balanced on the ice. But I thought about how if I mentioned it, she might fall down.

"Hey, Miss Becky." When Tara looked up into my eyes, I knew I was in for another one of her questions. "Is that boy you were talking to your boyfriend?"

I tugged on one of her blonde ringlets and watched it spring back into place.

"You know, young lady, I think you need to concentrate a little harder on your skating."

# Chapter 7

I had sixty dollars in my wallet. Two twenties and two tens. I'd deposited the rest of my pay into my savings account, then I'd gone downtown to try and spend my money. I took the metro to the Bay and wandered around there for a while. I stopped at the Mac makeup counter on the ground floor. I liked the Mac concealer, but there was still plenty left in my compact — even at the rate I used it.

Two girls were having their makeup done. One's eyelids flickered from the effort of keeping them closed. The other was smiling into a round mirror on the wall in front of her. You could tell she liked the way the makeup artist was turning her into someone else.

I thought of that line from *Snow White*: "Mirror, mirror on the wall, who's the fairest of them all?" And of the answer: "Why, you, of course."

No one would call me the fairest of them all. I ran my finger across my right cheek. It was still a little tender. I definitely wouldn't want some makeup lady touching my face, or peering at my skin through a magnifying glass.

I walked past cosmetics, and took the escalator to women's clothing on the second floor. Three salesgirls, probably university students working at the Bay for the summer, were chatting behind one of the cash registers.

I was glad when they didn't ask if I needed help. But when I passed them and they started giggling about some inside joke, I couldn't help feeling left out.

There was a party coming up for the camp staff. I hadn't decided if I wanted to go. I could always buy something new to wear — in case I went. I scanned the sales rack, but all the tops had short sleeves — or no sleeves at all.

It was only when I got to the shoe department that I realized there was nothing I wanted. Somehow, I'd had the feeling that buying something would make everything right — that I'd feel like that girl downstairs at the Mac counter smiling at her own reflection. But I realized now that no top, no makeup, no *anything*, could do that. The thought made me feel even worse.

Everywhere around me, people were walking purposefully through the aisles. They all seemed so sure of themselves, headed someplace important. Most were carrying shopping bags, and some had more than one. Why couldn't I be more like them?

When I walked out onto Ste-Catherine Street, the muggy late afternoon heat hit me like a soggy towel. Drivers honked their car horns, eager to get home and crank up their barbecues after a long day at the office.

I crossed the street to Phillips Square, where the street vendors were. You couldn't really call Phillips Square a park, and with only a few splotches of dried grass, it didn't exactly qualify as a green space either. A family of pigeons strutted along the asphalt path that led through the square, and a group of street kids were lying out on a faded red-and-white checked tablecloth. A tired-looking dog, its pink tongue hanging out of its mouth, held down the tablecloth at one end. Only the dog seemed to notice when I walked by, cocking his head to look in my direction.

I stopped to admire the sunflowers for sale at the first cart. Bright orange yellow, they were bigger than any sunflowers I'd ever seen, their black seedy centers the size of my hand.

"Je peux vous aider? Can I help you?" a man called from behind the cart. His skin was coppery from the sun.

"Non, merci."

The other carts sold mostly jewellery — baubles made of wire or silver, displayed on black velvet backgrounds. I stopped to look at a pair of silver earrings. I liked their triangular shape, the way they widened at the bottom.

I reached out to touch them, but at the last second, I pulled away. I didn't need earrings. I hardly ever wore the ones I had. Mom and Dad had given me pearl earrings two birthdays ago and they were still in their box in my top drawer.

A moment later, I spotted a bracelet. Because it was made of black leather that was hard to see against the velvet, I'd nearly missed it. But it was the crystal charm hanging on the bracelet that caught my eye — a small pear-shaped crystal no bigger than my thumbnail. It reminded me of ice, or maybe a teardrop. Either way, I liked it.

The woman standing by the cart gave me a friendly smile. I could tell she didn't want to scare me away, and risk losing a possible sale. Somehow, I had the feeling she'd been watching me since I'd crossed over into the small square.

"That's a very pretty bracelet," I told her, pointing at it. "Delicate." Yes, that was the right word for it.

"I made it."

I looked at her again. She was about my mom's age. All I could see of her hair were some silver strands at the temples. The rest was tied back in a blue bandanna. But somehow — and it wasn't just because she sold jewellery from a cart — you could tell she hadn't had an easy life. Maybe it was the wrinkles around her eyes, or the way her cheeks hung loosely on her face, like pillows that needed more stuffing.

"It's five dollars."

By then, I'd picked up the bracelet and laid it out in the palm of my hand.

"Try it on," she urged me.

"It's not for me."

I felt her eyeing my long sleeves. If she wondered why I was dressed like that on such a hot day, she didn't say anything.

"Do you have more?"

She reached for a cardboard box under her cart. "How many would you like?"

"Nine." I took my wallet out of my purse. "I teach skating. They're for the girls in my class."

I'd heard you could bargain with the street vendors, but five dollars seemed like a fair price. Besides, it didn't feel right to bargain with the person who'd made the bracelets. I handed her the two twenties and one ten-dollar bill.

She took my money, then reached for change into one of the pockets of her flowery apron. I watched as she counted out eight more bracelets. Was it the way the sun was shining through the maple trees — or were those pale lines running across the side of her wrist scars?

"Just a second. I have something for you." She reached into the box again, this time taking out a pile of neatly folded little bags that smelled of patchouli. She unfolded one to show it to me. Made of gauzy red material, it tied shut at one end with a gold ribbon.

"I made these too," she whispered.

"They're beautiful."

She put the gauzy bags and the bracelets into a plain brown bag, folding the end over.

"Making things helps," she said, almost as if she was talking to herself.

It seemed like a weird thing to say and for a second, I wondered if I'd heard her right.

"Excuse me?"

She looked me in the eye. "Making things helps."

I didn't know exactly what she'd meant, but I could tell she expected me to say something back. I tucked the brown bag under my arm.

"Thanks," I told her. "I'll try to remember that."

## Chapter 8

Mom was in the kitchen, talking on the phone about an open house.

"The house shows well," I heard her say. "It's well-maintained and the furnishings are fabulous — very contemporary — but the foundation worries me." She lowered her voice as if she was about to disclose some terrible secret. "There's a moldy smell downstairs. I told the owners to mask it with Febreeze. Just a second, Carole, I think my daughter just got home. Darling," she called out, "is that you?"

"Uh-huh," I called back as I kicked off my sneakers.

"I'm almost off the phone, Becks! Carole, let's talk tomorrow."

I rolled my eyes when Mom made a kiss-kiss noise into the receiver. She's always saying how she can't stand Carole, this other real estate agent in her office.

The house stank of nail-polish remover, which meant Errol was upstairs, gluing together one of his models with plastic cement.

*Making things helps.* The jeweller's words popped into my head. Maybe there was more to Errol's obsession with model airplanes than I'd realized.

From downstairs, I could see the door to his bedroom open up a crack. "Hey, Mom, you off the phone?" he shouted.

"Yes, dear," she called as she left the kitchen. I was "darling," Errol was "dear." Mom had an earphone wrapped around one ear, and the portable phone attached to her patent-leather belt. "Errol, if you're going to play that music of yours, just make sure it's not too loud. Okay, dear?"

It was too late. The music was already blaring. It was a miracle Errol wasn't totally deaf.

"So what did you buy?" Mom asked when she spotted the brown bag. She had to raise her voice so I could hear her.

"Just something for the girls at skating. Bracelets." I reached into the bag to show her one. "I met the woman who made them."

She took a quick look at the bracelet. She didn't seem impressed.

"Nothing for yourself? Wasn't today payday, darling?"

"There wasn't anything I wanted. Except the bracelets."

Mom gave me a look as if I was some rare species. "I don't know where you get it from, Becky. Certainly not from me. There's *always* "something I want," she added with a laugh.

"Look at it this way, Mom. You're good for the Canadian economy."

Mom had started flipping through the pile of mail on the bureau outside the kitchen.

"Speaking of stores and shopping, I ran into Beth Halliday's mother at the IGA. In the frozen food aisle, of all places. You know, when you freeze food, you lose some of the essential nutrients."

I nodded, hoping she wasn't going to go on about the nutrient thing again.

"Well," Mom continued, "she told me there's a party tomorrow night for all you camp counsellors. I think it's a wonderful idea. It'll give you a chance to meet new people. Maybe make some nice friends. You know, darling, we really should get you something new to wear. Something summery. You're always in such dark clothes. They just don't do you justice." She was tearing open an envelope, but I could feel her watching me from the corner of her eye.

I shifted from one foot to the other. Shopping with my mother was like having a tooth pulled. We had totally different taste. I liked plain. Mom liked sequins and ruffles. Plus she'd get insulted if I refused to try on something she picked out.

"That's okay," I told her. "Besides, I may not go."

"You should go, Becky." Mom had put the

envelope down on the bureau. You could tell she thought this was important because she'd stopped multi-tasking.

I decided it wasn't worth an argument. "I'll see," I told her.

I hadn't noticed Errol come downstairs. He was standing on the landing, watching us. He hadn't bothered to lower the music.

"What's for dinner?" When Errol spoke, it always sounded like he was shouting. Maybe the techno music *had* damaged his eardrums. And the plastic cement wasn't doing much for his personality, either.

Mom unclipped the portable phone from her belt and put it back on the cradle. "Salad and more salad," she said brightly. "I bought three kinds of lettuce today — romaine, iceberg, and curly red — and bean sprouts. There's nothing like roughage in your diet."

I interrupted her before she could start in about the functions of the small and large intestines. "Are we having any real food with our salad and more salad?" I asked.

Mom shook her head. You could tell she thought I just didn't get it.

"That sounds like the kind of question a fat person would ask." She curled her lip when she said the word "fat."

*Ouch*, I thought as I sucked in my breath. She hadn't called me fat, but she'd hinted at it. Not too subtly, either, which was just Mom's style.

Mom's face stiffened. "I'm sorry, Becks, I shouldn't have said that. It's just sometimes … I get so frustrated by how you let yourself go …"

"You're sick," Errol told her. He whispered, but the words came out like a hiss. "Can't you see what you're doing to her?"

"Errol! You're not to talk to me like that!" Mom's eyes shone, and for a second, I thought she was about to cry.

"I'm tired of you telling me what to do!" Now Errol was shouting. "You're the last person who should be giving anyone advice."

Mom was so angry she forgot to flip the hair away from her face.

"If you did what you were told, you might not have made such a mess of your life."

"Just stop it, the two of you! Stop it!" I didn't like Mom picking on me, but what was even worse was when she and Errol got into one of their fights.

I ran up to my room. I was relieved when I heard Errol come up the stairs behind me. At least, they weren't going to keep fighting. I shut my door and then, for good measure, I dragged my night table over to block the door.

"Becks." Mom was outside my door.

"Don't come in," I said, fighting back the tears.

"Becks, I'm really sorry. I didn't mean it."

The thing was: she had meant it. And she'd also meant what she'd said about Errol. That was why I was so upset. But there was no use telling her that. So I didn't say a word. I just lay on my bed, staring up at the ceiling.

I could hear her breathing outside my room. I didn't care if she never went away.

I rolled up my sleeve to the elbow and looked at my wrist. Crusty scabs had begun to form on the newest cuts. Behind them were the pale scars from older cuts.

I picked at one of the scabs with my fingernail. A bit of hard, dry scab flew into the air, landing on the floor. For a moment, the exposed skin, where the scab had been, felt as if it were on fire, but then the feeling passed.

The first dot of blood — bright red — made me want more. I picked harder, letting the nail dig a little deeper. I wasn't just after the gush of blood — I wanted … I needed … to feel pain.

When I got up from my bed, I had this weird sensation. Even though I'd taken down her poster when I'd stopped competing, I felt like Oksana Baiul was watching me. Shaking her head as I walked across the room to my desk.

But not even Oksana could stop me now.

When I reached down for my pencil tin, my eyes landed on my belly. It spilled over my low-rise jeans like a flesh-coloured tire. Disgusting. Mom was right. I was fat. No wonder I sounded like a fat person.

I felt the weight of the Swiss Army knife in my palm. I could still put it back in the pencil tin. Stop myself before I did any more damage. But the temptation was too strong. I needed the relief the knife could bring me. The numbness.

I flicked open the blade, sighing at the first flash of steel. This time, though, I didn't go back to my bed. Instead, I stepped towards the night table blockading the door. If I listened carefully, I could hear the sound of Mom's steady breathing.

Why didn't she go and apologize to Errol? What she'd said to him was just as bad — maybe even worse — than what she'd said to me.

Mom thought whatever was wrong with me could be fixed if I lost ten pounds. What she didn't know was I'd made a mess of my life, too. A big mess. Maybe it was more obvious in Errol's case because he'd dropped out of school. But the truth was, I wasn't doing much better than him. Even if no one could tell from the outside.

I sat down on the edge of the table and went to work, adding two fresh slices to the row of cuts on my wrist. The pain from the new cuts seemed to join with the pain from the open scabs. When I closed my eyes, I saw a bright silver flash, like lightning. So that was the colour of pain.

I used a Kleenex to catch the drips. I was careful not to get any blood on the bedspread. I knew from experience how hard it was to get rid of bloodstains. You have to scrub over and over at them with a cold soapy washcloth.

So that I wouldn't call out, I bit down as hard as I could on my lower lip. So hard I drew blood.

Finally, my body began to relax.

# Chapter 9

I don't know what I thought about for the next half-hour.

I just lay on my bed and zoned out. Like I was in some other world. A world that seemed oddly familiar — a place I'd visited ages ago — only I couldn't remember exactly when. I kept searching my mind for the answer, but it was like when you catch a whiff of some smell, someone's perfume or even grass after a rain shower, and it triggers a memory you can't quite place. No matter how hard you try.

The main thing was that while I was lying there, staring up at the ceiling, nothing bothered me. Nothing. Not Errol's techno music, or the sound of my mom hovering outside my door.

"Are you ready to come down for dinner, Becks?" she asked at one point.

I heard her voice, but it seemed to be coming

from very far away. Usually, I'd have been annoyed, but now I just lay on my bed and smiled. Besides, I was too zoned out to answer. Eventually, she went down the hall to talk to Errol, but I was too out of it to try and make out what they were saying. All I heard was a low mumble, like waves.

*What I'd give to feel like this forever,* I thought. Numb. Safe.

Even the two new slices on my wrist didn't bother me. I'd used more Kleenex to stop the bleeding and now my wrists just looked red and sore, like a slab of meat at the butcher's counter.

The balled-up pieces of Kleenex were on the floor by my bed. Later, I'd have to get rid of them. Destroy the evidence. I'd wait by the toilet until they were completely flushed away. But for now, I didn't want to think about later. I just wanted to keep floating for as long as I could.

Of course, I knew the feeling wouldn't last. In fact, lately, the zoned-out period seemed to be getting shorter every time I cut myself. But there was no point thinking about that now either. *Just relax, Becks*, I told myself. *Let yourself go*. And that's exactly what I did.

It didn't matter if I looked up at the ceiling, or over at the Scotch Tape marks on the wall, or down at my arm, or even at the pencil tin on my desk. I felt completely peaceful. I'd heard about yogis in India who got into such deep meditative states they could walk on burning coals without flinching. Maybe I was becoming like them. The thought made me smile.

I also knew from experience that the zoned-out feeling wouldn't go away all at once. It would fade, the way darkness comes on at the end of the day this time of year, a smoky greyness gathering at the edge of the horizon like storm clouds.

The first sign of that darkness was a dull ache in my wrist. Soon, it turned into a throb that kept time with my heartbeat — and with Errol's music. Then the repetitive throb of the techno music started to annoy me. I thought about asking Errol to turn it down, but then my mom, who probably thought I'd fallen asleep, would be back on my case. So instead, I stayed lying down, trying to get back to that place where nothing bothered me. I took a few long, deep breaths to calm myself. Maybe I really could be like a yogi.

Only the deep breaths didn't help. In fact, they seemed to be making things worse. I got up and sat at the corner of my bed, cradling the top of my head in my hands. Now the Kleenexes on the floor looked gross and disgusting. I had to get rid of them. And I had to put on some Neosporin. But I wasn't ready to leave my room. Not yet.

So I reached down for the tissues, gathering them up from the floor as if they were flowers. White ones with bright red splotches. Carnations, maybe. Or in the case of the ones that were almost completely soaked in blood, poppies. I'd always liked poppies. Poppies were for remembrance.

I scrunched the tissues up into a ball. I thought about stuffing them under my pillow, but I worried they might stain the sheets. That was just the sort of thing Mom would pick up with her X-ray vision. I put the ball of Kleenex near my door. Later, I'd hide it under my shirt, then flush it down the toilet.

My eyes landed on my sketchbook, on the floor near my door. Careful not to make too much noise, I got up from my bed and walked over to get it. Then I went back to where I'd been sitting and began flipping through the pages.

That skate I'd drawn wasn't any good. The proportions were all wrong. The blade too large for the skate, the lace, too long.

The drawing I'd done of Amy's mom wasn't any better. Her hair looked like a hat. I was a lousy artist. I wasn't an artist at all. Making things might help, but nothing I made was worth keeping.

I tugged at the inside corner of the page I was on, pulling the spiral binder taut, but then I let it go. I didn't have the strength to tear out the page. My wrist was throbbing too much. The spiral sprung back into place.

I'd used a night table to block the door, but there was a pencil on my other night table. I leaned over and reached for it. At first, I rolled the pencil between my fingers, finding comfort every time I reached one of its hard edges.

I opened the sketchbook to a fresh page, one I hadn't messed up yet with my lousy drawings.

Without planning to, I started drawing a poppy. On paper, it was black and white. But in my heart, it was bright red.

I tried to keep my wrist away from the page as I worked on the poppy's black centre. The dark thoughts came more quickly now. This time, they took the form of questions. *What was wrong with me? Why did I keep hurting myself? And why did hurting myself feel so good — at least for a short while after I'd done it?*

I pressed down harder on the page, so hard I nearly tore the paper. I knew I could Google "cutting," find out more about it. These days, you could find anything on the Net. But truth was, I didn't really want to know. Not yet.

I'd been making small dark squiggles for the centre of the poppy, but now the squiggles seemed to take on a life of their own, moving away from the flower and over to the parts of the page that were still blank.

Then, without planning it, I found myself writing words inside the squiggles. But somehow, the words didn't seem to be coming from the part of my brain that words usually come from. No, these words were like a cross between words and pictures. And they were coming quickly, almost too quickly for me to catch them and write them down.

This is what I wrote: "I shouldn't have done it. I shouldn't have done it. I shouldn't have. I must be crazy. Crazy. Crazy."

As my pencil moved more and more quickly, my wrist brushed against the page. The friction reopened the cuts, leaving behind a bloody trail.

# Chapter 10

"I'm delighted you decided to go to the party," Mom said as I was leaving the house. She was wearing a red sundress, so low-cut you could see the round tops of her breasts. Sometimes Mom dressed a little young for her age. Not that I'd ever tell her. Mom didn't like to be criticized. Not that that stopped her from dishing it out.

Dad was standing next to her on the porch, one arm around her waist. "You be safe now, Becky," he said, tapping me on the back with his free hand.

Mom was delighted, all right. So delighted she didn't even make any remarks about my outfit — a faded pair of jeans and a grey ribbed T-shirt — long-sleeved, of course.

I wasn't going to the party for her, I was going for me. To feel normal. I couldn't just doodle in my sketchbook all day, or lie on my bed, staring up at the ceiling like some zombie. So I hid the sketchbook under my mattress and tried to pull myself together. Maybe if I acted normal, I'd feel normal.

I thought about what I'd told my skaters: You have to learn to pick yourself up. What kind of instructor would I be if I couldn't follow my own advice?

The party was at Daphnée's, the new soccer instructor, the one Beth had been hanging out with at the canteen. Daphnée lived in a grey stone townhouse in lower Westmount, south of Sherbrooke Street. It was a nice neighbourhood, close to everything, including the metro, and way less snooty than upper Westmount.

I could have taken the bus or metro, but, in the end, I walked. I thought maybe walking would help clear my head. Actually, what I really needed was to get out of my head altogether. I couldn't help feeling I'd be happier if I was the kind of person who didn't think so much.

Even before someone answered Daphnée's door, I could tell her parents were out. The windows were closed, but loud music was coming from inside. At least it wasn't techno. I could see a couple of kids dancing on a table in the front room, their bodies swaying to the beat. Some guy I'd never seen before answered the door and the first thing I noticed was a thick cloud of cigarette smoke hovering in the air.

In the kitchen, every inch of counter and tabletop was covered in beer and liquor bottles, many of them already empty. Except for a few bowls of chips and pretzels, there was no food. Too bad, because, though we'd eaten barbecued chicken and salad (of course), for dinner, I was starving. I was beginning to think it wasn't just skating that gave me an appetite. Being anxious made me hungry, too.

Someone near me burped, leaving a yeasty smell in the air. Already, I regretted my decision to come. I checked my watch. 9:15. If I didn't want to seem antisocial, I'd have to stay until at least 10:30. And of course, if I got home too early, Mom would get crabby. I tried to weigh what was worse: staying here and feeling like I didn't belong, or going home and facing Mom.

The place was so jammed I didn't really get to decide where I wanted to go next. It was more like the weight of bodies was pushing me out of the kitchen and into the next room, which turned out to be the den. The walls were covered in dark wood panelling and in the background, Busta Rhymes was singing "Touch It": *Touch it, bring it, buy it...* My shoulders swayed with the music.

Someone reached into a cooler and handed me a bottle of Mike's Hard Lemonade. Droplets of cool water trickled down my sleeve. Good thing I was a righty. Otherwise, I'd have had to use the other arm. The water would have collected near the Band-Aids on my wrist. Made them soggy, itchy.

The den was way less crowded than the kitchen. I took a gulp of the lemonade, then another. Maybe alcohol would help me get outside my head. I couldn't taste the booze, but at least I could breathe in here. A bunch of kids were sitting on an L-shaped couch. At first, all I saw were their backs. Until one of them turned around.

"Hey Becky," a voice called out. It was Tory.

I don't know why I felt surprised to see him. I'd spent most of the walk over imagining running into him at the party and what we might say to each other: "So fill me in on the last six years," and, "Have you kept in touch with any of your old hockey friends — the ones who used to call me 'Ice Princess'?"

But still, somehow, I was surprised. It was like when I'd first run into him at camp — this feeling of the past and present colliding in some totally unexpected way. Like two planets spinning out of orbit. The thought made me slightly dizzy. It couldn't be the hard lemonade, could it? I'd only had two swigs.

Tory raised his beer bottle in the air as if he was making a toast. Then he slid over on the couch to make room for me.

For a moment, I hesitated.

Then I spotted Beth. She was sitting on the other end of the L.

"Beck-y!" The way she said my name, dragging out the "y" at the end, made it sound like she was glad to see me. Or drunk. Probably drunk.

"Hey, Becky," she said, "I meant to tell you what I heard the girls in your group say about you."

I felt my legs stiffen. I hoped it wasn't something about my makeup — or even worse, about Tory.

"What'd they say?" I mumbled, as I sat down in the spot Tory had made for me. I hoped Beth couldn't tell I was nervous.

"They said you don't just teach them skating. They said you teach them about real life, too. Pretty deep for seven-year-olds, no?" It didn't sound like Beth was teasing me, but I wasn't sure. And even from where I was sitting, I could tell she smelled of beer.

I shrugged — in case she was teasing me. "I bet they were just trying to be nice."

"No they weren't." Tory sounded annoyed. "What is it about you, Becky, that you can't take a compliment?"

I shrugged again. I'd only been at the party for ten minutes and already I was screwing things up. Tory was right. Why couldn't I take a compliment? For a second, I imagined smiling graciously and saying, "Thank you very much, Beth, for telling me that." But even to my own ears, the words didn't sound right — not coming from me.

A guy with spiky blue hair and a pierced eyebrow had his hand on Beth's knee.

"Have you met Steve?" she asked, when she caught me looking at him. Steve nodded in my direction. "He does trampoline," Beth explained.

That cracked Steve up, though I didn't see what was so funny. When Steve finally stopped laughing, he started rubbing the side of Beth's thigh.

"So Mr. Trampoline Man, you gonna roll another joint, or what?" someone else asked.

Steve used his other hand to pull a rolled up baggie from the front pocket of his jeans.

"I'm glad you came to the party," Tory whispered. His breath felt hot against my ear.

Once he rolled the joint, Steve put it between Beth's lips and lit it.

"Aren't you a gentleman?" she said, after she took a puff. Tory's turn was next. I watched to see what he'd do. I'd smoked up once before, but nothing had happened. To be honest, I didn't see what all the fuss was about.

Tory took a long drag on the joint. Then he passed it to me, and plunked down on the pillows behind him, his eyes barely shut.

*What the hell*, I thought. So I went ahead and took a puff, holding it in for as long as I could before exhaling. The smoke tickled my lungs. When the joint came around a second time, I had another puff.

The first thing I noticed was how my tongue felt thick and heavy, as if it was stuck at the bottom of my mouth. I reached for my Hard Lemonade. As I leaned forward towards the coffee table, the bottle suddenly seemed to get very large, so that it took up my entire field of vision. I leaned backward, just to see what would happen. This time, the bottle got so small it was just a speck. Did that mean I was stoned? The whole thing cracked me up. Soon, the others were laughing, too.

Tory's leg brushed against mine. For a second, I wondered what it would feel like to have his hand on my thigh.

It suddenly struck me that I was having fun. Me, Becky Sanger, having fun at a camp party. That made me laugh even more. Only now, my laughter seemed to be coming from very far away.

Just then, I sensed a shadow moving behind me, and all at once, someone grabbed the top of my arm, pinching the soft flesh that was there.

"C'mon, Janie, let's dance," a strange voice called out, pulling me up from the couch without letting go of my arm.

Tory jumped up from where he'd been sitting.

"Hey man," he said. "Let go of her! Her name's not Janie."

But by then, it was too late. The room was spinning, the objects around me — the table, a television, the books on a nearby shelf — were so big I was afraid they might crush me.

At first, I was frozen, but then I began to shake, and a moment later, the tears came. More tears than I'd ever imagined. A waterfall of tears. It was all so embarrassing, but there didn't seem to be anything I could do to stop the waterfall — or the shaking.

"Lookit," the strange voice sounded nervous now, speaking very quickly. "All I did was grab your arm. Hey, I'm really sorry. I didn't mean anything by it. I thought you were Janie."

# Chapter 11

The toilet wobbled when I sat down. I'd made a run for the bathroom, the crowd parting to clear a path for me, the way drivers pull off to the side of the road when they hear an ambulance siren. They probably thought I was going to be sick all over Daphnée's parents' beige carpeting.

I flicked the lock on the bathroom door and tried to catch my breath. I had the feeling Tory might be on the other side of the door — I was pretty sure he'd followed me from the den — but if he was there, he wasn't saying anything. With the loud music in the background, I couldn't exactly listen for someone's breathing.

I dropped my head to my knees. At first, I kept my eyes closed, but when I opened them, I noticed how some of the small black-and-white tiles near the base of the toilet were cracked. And how there were bits of black dirt trapped in the cracks.

I shut my eyes again. What was it about that guy grabbing my arm that had upset me so much? I could still feel the throbbing in my upper arm, about halfway between my shoulder and my elbow. The throbbing was so strong I wondered whether I was misjudging this sensation, too — in the same way as the objects in the living room had seemed so much bigger than usual.

The weirdest part was that it was as if the tissue in my upper arm contained a memory — a memory that was triggered when that boy had tried to pull me off the sofa. Yet I couldn't place the memory. Only the throbbing in my arm seemed familiar.

I heard a burping sound, but it took me a few seconds to realize I was the one who'd made it. The air in the bathroom felt warm and heavy, like the air in a sauna, and it smelled sour, like lemonade. I thought about opening the window or going over to the sink and splashing my face with cold water, but I was afraid I might fall over if I tried to stand up.

And then, all at once, when I'd stopped trying, I remembered. It felt as if I'd found a missing piece to a jigsaw puzzle but that the piece had been there all along, wedged in the corner of the box.

Someone long long ago had tugged on my arm. She'd tugged many times, way harder than this strange boy had tugged my arm tonight. She'd tugged so hard she'd sometimes left marks. An arc of purple-blue fingerprints like one of those armband tattoos.

*Zofia.* Why was it that even thinking her name made me wince?

Zofia Lupescu had been my skating coach. The skating coach Mom and Dad had convinced to train me. A former elite athlete herself, Zofia was going to take me all the way to the Olympics. Whatever it took.

I winced again.

And now I suddenly remembered how when I fell, or when I didn't skate fast enough for her liking, Zofia would grab me by the arm, the same arm that hurt so much now. Maybe my body really did have a memory of its own.

"Her methods are a little unconventional, but think how lucky Becky is to be working with an Olympic athlete." That's what Mom told Dad after she noticed the bruising. At the time, I didn't know what the word "unconventional" meant, but I was smart enough to know Mom wasn't going to stand up for me.

"Who did that to you?" Mom had asked when she first saw the fingermarks on my arm. I'd been getting out of the tub and Mom was kneeling on the floor, a fluffy towel in her arms.

"Zofia," I'd told her, looking down at the floor.

Zofia could do no wrong in Mom's eyes. Not if she was going to take me to the Olympics.

Why hadn't I said anything? Why hadn't I told my parents how cruel Zofia was? And why hadn't I ever told Zofia to stop?

Of course I knew the answers. I wasn't brave

enough. Zofia wore me out. She broke me. And Mom was so star-struck, so excited about the possibility of my going to the Olympics, she'd never have done anything to stop Zofia. As for Dad … well Dad basically went along with whatever Mom thought was right.

The memory of those bruises on the outside of my arm gave me a sick feeling in my stomach and filled me with a terrible sadness. The strange thing was I wasn't sad for who I was now; I was sad for who I'd been. A little girl. A helpless little girl who didn't know how to stand up for herself.

It was only when I started to cry that I heard Tory's voice.

"Becky!" he said, loud enough so I'd hear him over the music. "Let me in."

"No," I said between sniffles.

"I think you had too much weed. You're probably not used to it."

In a weird way, I was glad to have Tory's company, even though we were separated by the bathroom door.

"Come on out," he urged me.

Someone pounded on the door. "Hey, I really need to pee," a girl's voice said.

"Look, a friend of mine's in there," I heard Tory explain. "She needs a little time. Isn't there another bathroom upstairs?"

"Someone's in that one, too."

I wiped away my tears with the back of my hand and cleared my throat. "It's okay," I called out, "I'm nearly done." I flushed the toilet to give myself a little more time. Then I washed my hands. To the right of the sink, I spotted a razor blade on a glass shelf. Why hadn't I noticed it before? My eyes lingered on the sharp edge.

"Can you speed it up, *please*?" the girl said.

When I let myself out, Tory threw his arm around my shoulders.

His eyes were bloodshot. "Let's go find someplace quiet," he said.

I let myself lean on his arm as he led me upstairs, but then I backed away. "You're not taking me to some bedroom, are you?" I knew I was blushing.

Tory gave me a lopsided grin. "What do you think I am — some kind of pervert? There's another den upstairs and I'm hoping no one's there. Not so we can make out. Just so you can relax."

The room he took me to was more like a library than a den. There were floor-to-ceiling bookshelves on all four walls. Tory sat me down on a brown leather couch.

"You feeling better?" he asked, kneeling in front of me. I felt his pale eyes on my face. He was probably hoping I wouldn't start crying all over again.

I cleared my throat. "When that guy grabbed my arm, it reminded me of something … of someone …."

"Who?" Tory asked, without lifting his eyes from my face.

76

That's when I realized Tory might remember Zofia. He'd played hockey at the same rink in east-end Montreal where I'd trained with her.

"Do you remember this coach I had … Zofia?" Just saying her name was hard for me.

"Little lady? Short black hair? Army sergeant type?"

I hadn't thought of Zofia in ages, and now, when I pictured her, my arm hurt even more. "That's her," I told Tory. "I guess she was pretty tough on me. It's weird that I haven't thought of her in so long."

Tory nodded. "It's not that weird. Maybe you were trying to block her out. I mean, because she gave you such a hard time. I remember she yelled a lot."

"Yelling was the least of it," I whispered. I rubbed my forehead with the palms of my hands.

Tory stroked his chin. "I never had a good feeling about that woman. Even when I was a kid."

That made me feel a little better. At least someone else had noticed.

"Listen, can I get you some water or something?" Tory asked. He'd gotten up from the floor by then. I'd have liked to tell him I just wanted him nearby, but I didn't want to embarrass him — or me.

There was a bathroom in the hallway, outside the second-floor den, and I heard Tory running the water.

Maybe he was right. Maybe I had been trying to block Zofia out of my mind. I wished I could block her out right now, but I couldn't. I kept picturing her face — she had sharp features that had always reminded me of a bird. A small bird that moved quickly and pecked a lot.

And then I remembered the hard rubber arch supports she'd forced me to wear. She said it was because I had flat feet. *"Skaters need arches,"* I heard her say in my mind. I thought I'd die from the pain of wearing those things. But she'd made me wear them every single time I got on the ice.

I shut my eyes, hoping the memory would go away.

But it wouldn't. Zofia had made me wear those arch supports even after I showed her the bottoms of my feet, covered in open blisters.

Mom must have seen the blood when she did the laundry. But she'd never said anything about it. Not a word.

I had to go home. I had to be in my room.

"Tory!" I called out, as I got up from the couch. "I really need to go."

Of course, I had a pretty good idea of what I'd do once I got to my room.

# Chapter 12

"Did your parents explain why we thought it might be a good idea for you to come here today, Becky?" Dr. Sewell peered at me from behind his thick glasses. He'd moved his chair to the front of his desk so the five of us were sitting in a circle, with Mom and Dad on the couch across from him, and Errol and I in two hard chairs on either side. Dr. Sewell had a silver pen between his fingers and he was balancing a notepad on one knee.

"Not really," I told him, squirming a little in my seat.

"That's not exactly true," my mom piped in. "We told her how —"

Dad sighed. "Let him talk to Becky," he said in a sharper voice than he usually used with my mom.

Mom crossed her feet as if she thought that might help her stop interrupting. Errol winked at me. And that was just the first forty seconds of family counselling.

"We thought it might be useful to get your perspective on how things are going at home, Becky." Dr. Sewell flashed me a big smile. There was a droopy-looking miniature palm tree on the filing cabinet next to his desk. Underneath the palm tree were framed photographs of Dr. Sewell's family — three children and a red-haired wife. Perfectly well-adjusted, of course. I bet his kids didn't smoke dope at parties ... or have weird flashbacks ... or cut themselves.

Dr. Sewell was still smiling at me. For a second, I was worried he might be able to tell what I was thinking. *Relax*, I told myself, *the guy's a shrink, not a mind reader*.

Mom gave Errol a dirty look when he started rocking on the back legs of his chair.

Errol kept rocking. Mom bit her lip.

"Sure," I told Dr. Sewell, "I'd like to be helpful."

"I'd like to be helpful," Errol muttered under his breath.

This time, Dad shot him a dirty look. "Cut it out, will you?" Dad said.

I watched Dr. Sewell's eyes dart between Errol and my dad, but then, instead of saying anything to them, he turned back to me.

"How does it feel to be here today with us, Becky?"

For a second, I wondered if there was a right answer, and if I got it, if that would mean I'd never have to come back to this cramped little office and sit through another one of these unbearable sessions.

"It feels fine," I lied.

"Really, Becky?" Dr. Sewell's thick eyebrows rose behind his glasses and knit themselves together until they made one furry eyebrow that reminded me of a squirrel's tail.

"Okay, it feels a little weird."

Dr. Sewell smiled again. "Weird can be good," he said. "Sometimes, we feel weird when we're adjusting to new situations. New ways of dealing with things."

Here, he stopped to look at each of us, as if he wanted to be sure we got his message. Mom and Dad looked serious. Errol was staring at the floor.

"At any rate, Becky," Dr. Sewell continued, "we appreciate your joining us today." Then he lifted his pen so it was ready to write. "Maybe you could tell me a little about yourself, Becky."

He seemed to be making a point of using my name every time he talked to me. Probably some trick he'd learned at shrink school. Personally, I thought it was annoying. Which was when I got the idea of using the trick back on him.

I took a deep breath. "There isn't much to tell, Dr. Sewell. I've got a summer job teaching skating at a sports camp. I really enjoy working with kids."

Dr. Sewell's pen made scratching noises on the page.

Mom's lips were pursed. Then she let out a sigh. I got the feeling she might burst if she didn't get to say what she was thinking.

"Becky's totally devoted to those girls," she said at last. "Totally devoted."

Errol made a snorting sound.

Dr. Sewell turned to Errol. "Do you have a problem with your sister's summer employment, Errol?" There, he'd done it again, saying Errol's name at the end of his sentence.

"I don't give a crap about her summer em-ploy-ment," Errol said, shrugging his shoulders and dragging out the word "employment" the way Dr. Sewell had done. If Dr. Sewell noticed that Errol was now imitating him, he didn't let on.

Mom winced. "Do you have to use that language?" I don't know why Mom was acting so prissy. Errol used words like "crap" all the time.

Dad gave Mom another look, as if to say that if she interrupted one more time he'd never clear another dinner dish.

"I'm sensing some hostility in you, Errol." He didn't need to go to shrink school to figure that one out.

Errol snorted again, only louder this time.

"Look, Doc," he said. "It's not all that hard to figure out, is it? Becky's Little Miss Perfect — "totally devoted" to those girls she works with — and me, I'm the asshole. Every family's got to have one."

Little Miss Perfect. Boy, that was a laugh! And

82

did Errol ever have it wrong! In his eyes, I might be perfect, but I knew better than anyone: I was Little Miss Imperfect. I dropped my eyes to my thighs. The seams of my jeans were pulling at the top. Correction: *Big* Miss Imperfect.

"Is that really how you think of yourself, Errol — as the family asshole?" Dr. Sewell made the word "asshole" sound like a medical condition.

Usually Errol had a quick answer for everything, but this time, he actually seemed to be thinking about Dr. Sewell's question. "Well, it's what *they* think about me." Errol's eyes were fixed on Dr. Sewell's wood floor, but I knew he was talking about my parents.

"I see," Dr. Sewell said. "That's actually a very astute psychological observation, Errol. It's not unusual for members of families to take on certain roles and to be perceived in a certain way."

I'd have liked to say he was right about Errol taking on the role of asshole, but of course, I didn't. There was no point in getting everyone even more upset. But then I started wondering if the real reason I didn't say it was because I was taking on my role of Little Miss Perfect — always wanting to fix things and stop people from getting into fights.

Could I be pretending to be someone I wasn't? Which got me wondering if maybe Errol wasn't really an asshole — though, of course, in his case, he usually was.

This time, Dr. Sewell must have known what I was thinking, because he asked, "How does

Errol's description of you as Miss Perfect make you feel, Becky?"

"Little Miss Perfect," I said, correcting him. "Only I'm not so little."

That cracked Errol up.

"Errol, laughing like that is very unkind," Mom said.

"You should talk. You're the one who's always nagging her about her weight."

Dr. Sewell's eyes were moving so fast you'd think he was watching tennis.

"Your mom wants the best for the two of you," my dad said. This was the second time he'd broken his own rule about not interrupting.

Dr. Sewell turned to my mom. He smiled at her, but I could tell he was about to lob her a tough question. Now I felt like I was the one watching tennis. And to be honest, it was getting kind of exciting. We never got to talk to each other this way. There was something fun about it, but also something dangerous. As if one of us might go too far, say too much. Be too honest.

"Mrs. Sanger," Dr. Sewell said, "do you think your wanting the best for your children might be perceived by them, perhaps, in some way, as ..." he paused for a moment, "... criticism?"

*Oh my,* I thought. *Mom's not going to like this.* Still, I wanted to see how she'd react.

Her face had turned pale.

"Well," she said, uncrossing and then recrossing her ankles, "I certainly hope not."

"You can be pretty tough on them," my dad said.

"Edward!" Mom poked Dad with her elbow. "Are you turning on me now, too?"

"Is that how it feels to you, Mrs. Sanger?" Dr. Sewell asked.

Errol leaned forward in his chair. "Why do you think Becky hangs out in her room so much? It's because she can't handle being around you."

Though my mom had it coming, I was starting to feel sorry for her.

"That's not exactly true," I said.

Mom gave me a weak smile, the kind you give after you've had the flu and your appetite is starting to come back.

"So you hang out a lot in your room, Becky?" Dr. Sewell asked, raising his squirrel tail. Was it my imagination or was he staring at my long sleeves?

"I like to draw," I said, a little too quickly.

One thing about fifty minutes of family counselling is that it goes by really fast. But by the end of it, I felt like we'd been through a war. And my neck was aching from having to spin my head around so much.

When the session finally ended, Dr. Sewell made a point of shaking my hand. "It was good of you to join us, Becky," he said.

This time, it definitely wasn't my imagination, he was eyeing my wrists. "I hope you'll feel free to come back ... should you ever need to talk."

I tried to look right at him when I answered. "It was nice meeting you, Dr. Sewell, and thanks for the offer. But I'm doing fine. Just fine. Thank you very much."

After Dad wrote out a cheque and left it on Dr. Sewell's desk, I followed my parents and Errol out of the office. As I was leaving, I turned back for a second. Dr. Sewell was adding something to his notes.

"Your palm tree needs water," I told him. "Dr. Sewell."

# Chapter 13

I stopped Tory as he headed into the locker room. His campers were trailing behind him in single file, their hockey sticks tucked inside their elbows, exactly the way Tory was holding his stick. For a second, I remembered these ducklings I'd once seen crossing a road in the Laurentian Mountains, about an hour north of Montreal. They'd been following their mom, though now I wondered if it might've been their dad.

"Hey, have you got an old hockey stick I can borrow?" I called out.

When he turned around, Tory was smiling.

"Hey, Becky. How ya doin'? I wanted to check on you over the weekend — see how you were doing after I got you home …" he shot me a look. ".. only your phone number's not listed."

Now his campers were looking at me, too. If it were my girls, they'd have giggled when he said that about my phone number, but Tory's kids just leaned into their hockey sticks. Again, they were imitating Tory.

"I'm okay," I said, forcing a smile. I didn't like the idea of Tory worrying about me. "Thanks for asking. And for looking after me the other night. So, have you got a stick?"

I could feel Tory studying my face. I had the feeling he wanted to ask me something, but in the end, all he said was, "Sure, I'll bring one right out." Then he turned back to his campers.

"Hey, guys! Skates off! I want you guys in shorts and sneakers. We're going to do some endurance training. That is, if you want to win the Stanley Cup someday."

"Think we really might win the Stanley Cup?" I heard one boy ask his friend as they disappeared into the locker room.

My own campers were at Arts & Crafts, making mosaic picture frames, so I waited outside the boy's locker room. I hated having nothing to do, even if it was only for a few minutes. When I didn't have anything to do, my mind went places I didn't want it to go. To keep myself busy, I scanned the bulletin board, which was covered with ads for used sports equipment.

I arranged my hair so it would hide my right cheek. The gashes were almost healed, and I'd only had to apply a thin layer of foundation that morning. Then I ran my tongue across my lips to see if I still had any lip gloss on. None left, so I licked my lips instead. After that, I smiled, the way I planned to smile when Tory came out with the hockey stick. A little smile, not one of those wide ones that works your jaw muscles.

I had a feeling Tory was going to ask for my phone number, and I was trying to decide whether to give it to him. I wasn't sure I wanted him calling me up at home, maybe even asking me out on a date, but then I remembered how he'd waited outside the bathroom for me on Saturday night, and how he'd gone to get me water.

But when someone came rushing out of the locker room with a hockey stick, it wasn't Tory. It was one of his campers. "Here ya go," he said, handing me the stick.

"Tory said to say he's helping this kid named Scott unlace his skates."

"Thanks a lot." If it had been one of the girls in my group, she'd have been able to tell I was disappointed.

***

I'd already arranged a couple of hula hoops, three orange pylons, and a stray glove from the lost and found on the ice. Now I added the hockey stick, placing it between the last pylon and the glove.

Randy was the first to turn up after Arts & Crafts.

"My mosaic came out stupid-looking," she complained. "I'm throwing it out." I was about to tell her how making things is good for you, even when they don't turn out exactly how you planned, but by then she'd spotted all the stuff on the ice.

"Hey, is that an ox-stacle course?" she wanted to know.

I tried not to laugh. By then, the other girls had arrived and were clamoring to get out on the ice.

"Randy guessed it. You ladies are doing an obstacle course this morning. Here's how it works: You have to step in and then out of the hula hoops, skate around the pylons, walk over the hockey stick, and pick up the glove at the end. Got all that?"

Even Tara, who had finally begun to get her balance on the ice, wanted to get a turn. "It looks fun," I heard her tell one of the other girls.

Only Amy didn't seem excited. As usual, she was the first on the ice, but once again, she was practicing her stroking on the other side of the rink, far away from where I'd set up the obstacle course.

I cupped my hands over my mouth so she'd hear me better. "Amy!" I called out. "Come back here! I need you to go first."

Instead of coming back when I called her, Amy made one last circle around the rink.

"Is something bugging you today, Ame-ster?" I asked when she finally came skating over.

"It's too easy," she muttered, without looking up at me.

She'd thrown her shoulders back and though I couldn't see all of her face, the corners of her mouth were set in a pout.

"You're right," I told her, "it *is* too easy for you. So we're going to make things a little more challenging, but only for you."

Amy lifted her dark eyes from the ice. I could tell she was excited.

"What do you want me to do?"

"The other girls only have to step into the hula hoops. But because you're such a strong skater, you're going to *jump* into them. And you're going to jump over the hockey stick, too."

"Okay," Amy said, looking out at the ice. I knew she was studying the obstacle course, mapping out her route.

"My legs are stiff today," I told the other girls. "So Amy's going to demonstrate."

They watched as Amy jumped in and out of the hula hoops, slalomed through the pylons, jumped over the hockey stick, and finally, swooped down to pick up the glove. Within a minute, she was back, sliding to a halt as she handed me the glove.

"Nice work," I told her, "very nice." Then I turned to the rest of the class. "I'm not expecting the rest of you to do the obstacle course quite so quickly — and you're going to step and in and out of the hula hoops, not jump like Amy did. The whole idea is for you girls to keep working on your balance — and on skating forwards."

I skated over to the end of the obstacle course and tossed the glove back onto the ice. "Okay, Randy," I called out. "Show us your moves!"

I waited at the end of the course, where I could keep an eye on the girls as they went through it. "We want to do it again!" several of them called out after they'd each had a turn.

When Tara fell, it happened so fast there wasn't anything I could do. She hadn't managed to clear the hockey stick. Instead, the blade on one of her skates landed on the stick's surface. It was a good thing she hadn't been going quickly, but the fall must have hurt more than her feelings, because she landed smack on her back.

"Are you okay, honey?" I called out as I rushed over to her.

Tara's eyes were wet with tears, but she didn't complain. "My bum hurts," was all she said as she picked herself up from the ice. I clapped her back to loosen the frost from her navy sweatshirt.

I made the other girls wait by the boards while I took Tara to the camp nurse's office.

"You'll be fine," the nurse, Marcy, assured Tara. "We're going to let you lie down. And we'll give you a little ice for your bruise."

"I don't know if Tara can handle any more ice today," I joked. When Tara laughed, I figured that meant I could go back to the other girls.

"Tara's going to be fine," I told them when I got back to the rink. "But I think that's enough obstacle course work for one day." Truth was, I didn't think I could handle another one of them taking a spill.

"We'll spend the rest of today's session working on forward skating. Let's start by circling around the rink together."

Of course, Amy was on her third lap when most of the girls were still finishing up their first. When she passed me, I picked up my pace and caught up with her. There was no question about it — the girl needed an accelerated skating program.

I started doing crosscuts, leaning into the middle of the rink and raising my right foot over my left. Amy slowed down to watch.

"Amy," I said as I waited for her to catch up with me, "how would you like to learn to do backwards crosscuts?"

She nodded her head yes.

"You're a really good skater," I told her as I extended her right arm forward, and her left arm backward. Then, because I didn't want her front arm to drift, I got her to rest her palm on mine. "Now all you've got to do is balance on your left foot. Like this …"

I shouldn't have been surprised by how quickly she caught on.

At the end of the session, Amy's cheeks were rosy from all her hard work. I'd been right about her needing a more advanced program. Maybe I'd speak to her mom about private lessons.

But as it turned out, I didn't need to. Mrs. Gross intercepted me outside the rec centre that afternoon. "I'm trying to arrange a private skating coach for Amy," she told me, her voice a little breathless. I couldn't see her eyes because she was wearing huge purple-tinted sunglasses with rhinestones at the corners.

"That's great news," I told her. " I was thinking how —"

Mrs. Gross didn't wait for me finish my sentence. "The coach I've been in touch with sounds just marvelous. She actually competed in the Olympics."

A she? Who competed in the Olympics?

I felt my heart sink. *Don't let it be Zofia*, I thought.

"Well, she's agreed to meet Amy. We're hoping you can help her prepare for the audition. We'll pay you, of course. An Olympic athlete! You can imagine how excited we are! Oh, I almost forgot to tell you, the coach mentioned she knew you. You do remember Zofia Lupescu?"

# Chapter 14

I don't know why I didn't say anything to Mrs. Gross. All I did was nod like one of those bobble-head dolls when she told me the news that there's a chance that Amy will be training with Zofia Lupescu. It was as if the words got stuck in my throat, and even now, I could still feel them lodged there, making it hard for me to swallow.

Zofia Lupescu! I hadn't heard her name in ages. And until I smoked up at Daphnée's party, I hadn't thought of Zofia in ages, either. I'd thought all those dark days were behind me. But now it felt like Zofia was back in my life — tormenting me just like she used to.

Zofia had told me once, proudly, how the name "Lupescu" came from the Romanian word for wolf. I didn't have the courage to tell her what I thought: that with her long straight nose, dark eyes, and most of all, her fiery temper, she could easily be a wolf. A big, bad she-wolf. One who preyed on helpless girls like the one I used to be. Girls so determined to make it as competitive skaters, they'd put up with her abuse.

I couldn't bear the idea of her doing that to Amy. But what could I do to stop it? Who would listen to me? Certainly not Amy's mother. No, she wouldn't take me seriously if I told her how cruel Zofia could be. Mrs. Gross was just like my mom. And though Mom's mantra was that she wanted the best for me, I knew the truth: she'd have fed me to the wolves if that could have made me a star. And her the mother of a star. Even if it meant blisters and bruises … and blood.

When I got back to my room I felt like I was being flooded by memories of Zofia. There didn't seem to be anything I could do to stop the flood.

Mostly, I remembered little things, but somehow they made me even sadder than thinking about the hard rubber arch supports and Zofia's handprint on my arm.

It's as if Zofia Lupescu had taken something away from me — something I'd never been able to get back since the days she was my coach.

I remembered how when the skating rink shut down at lunch so the Zamboni guy could resurface the ice, I'd sit with Zofia. I'd eat the lunch Mom packed: cubes of cheddar cheese, celery and carrot sticks, an apple, maybe a banana. Zofia would order hot dogs and french fries from the canteen. But only for herself. She'd douse it all with ketchup as if the ketchup was gasoline and she wanted to start a fire. I could still picture the ketchup oozing out of the tiny rectangular foil wrapper.

One time, I got up from the green plastic table where I had been sitting across from Zofia, and walked over to the canteen. Mom had given me money after I complained how her lunches didn't give me enough energy to skate all day. I'd been barely tall enough to see over the counter, so I'd stood on my toes.

"A hot dog and an order of fries, please," I'd told the man who took people's orders.

Zofia had leapt up from her chair. Her eyes had flashed like lightning. "Are you crazy or zum-zing?" she had shouted. "You're not allowed to eat zat junk. Cancel her order this instant," she had told the man. And of course, he'd listened to her. That's when I'd learned that people like Zofia — people who frighten others — usually get their way.

Of course, Zofia could eat all the junk she wanted. I'd just watched her polish off her lunch, licking her lips afterwards and using the back of her hand to rub the ketchup from the side of her mouth. Like a wolf. Sometimes, she'd order another hot dog, and she'd watch me watching her eat it. Even back then, I knew she was enjoying the power she had over me.

Once, when Zofia went to make a phone call, I'd just stared at the tiny specks of crumbs left on her plastic plate. It was like they'd had some kind of hypnotic power over me. Some torn-open envelopes of ketchup were lying in a pile at the edge of the plate. I could smell their salty-sweet scent. And then, when I just couldn't take it anymore — the churning in my stomach, the frustration of not being able to eat what I wanted and of having had to watch Zofia stuff herself — I'd reached for one of the packets of ketchup and squeezed what was left of it into my mouth. There couldn't have been more than a few drops left, but I devoured them, like a vampire sucking blood. Luckily, Zofia didn't catch me. Not that time.

*You useless bitch!*

I could almost hear Zofia talking to me. Saying those awful words. That was what she used to call me when I did something wrong, or when I wasn't quick enough, or when I got frustrated trying to learn a new move.

*You useless bitch!*

What kind of thing was that to say to a nine-year-old?

She'd been teaching me the axel jump. I'd mastered the single rotation, so I was ready for the axel. I'd always been a good jumper. I could jump two, maybe two-and-a-half feet in the air, but I'd had to relearn my timing for the axel. Instead of a single rotation, I now had to turn one-and-a-half times.

Zofia had skated over to the center of the rink to demonstrate the move.

"You take off from the edge of your skate, not from zee toe pick," she'd explained.

The axel had been way harder than it looked. At first, I couldn't get the timing. So I'd kicked the ice. Hard. I was being a baby, but hey, I was only nine. What had Zofia expected of me?

"You useless bitch!" Zofia shouted. I didn't know what the word "bitch" meant, but I could tell Zofia was angry and that I'd done something really bad.

"I'm sorry," I'd muttered under my breath, fighting back the tears. My arms and legs shook, the way they always did when Zofia lost her temper. Mom and Dad had gone to a lot of trouble to get Zofia to be my coach. I'd been lucky she'd agreed to take me on as a pupil. I'd known I shouldn't upset her. But Zofia had a short fuse.

I never knew what might set her off. It could be the smallest thing — like if I complained my legs were tired.

Sometimes, she'd stomp off the ice, slamming the door to the stands behind her.

I'd be left alone on the ice, lost without my coach. Of course, I knew what I'd have to do next, because it was always the same. I'd have to go after her — and apologize some more: "I'm really really sorry, Zofia. I should never have said my legs were tired. They're not tired anymore. Not tired at all. Please give me another chance. Please, Zofia! Please!"

She'd wanted me to beg. And that's exactly

what I'd done. Remembering all this was making me feel sick to my stomach.

ZOPHIA WAS THE USELESS BITCH.

NOT ME!

\*\*\*

I was too angry to draw, too angry to lie on my bed.

I trudged over to my desk. I could've reached over into my pencil tin for the Swiss Army knife. But I didn't.

Not because I didn't feel like cutting. No, it wasn't that at all.

It was because this time, I knew cutting wouldn't be enough to numb my feelings. No, this time, the feelings were much too strong.

I felt like a robot as I walked downstairs to the kitchen. I could picture exactly what I was about to do. I was going to turn on the front burner on the stove, let it heat up until it glowed nice and orange. Then I'd take a spoon out of the cutlery drawer and hold it against the burner. And then, when the spoon was burning hot, smoking even, I'd press it down against my wrist.

Once I'd turned the burner on, I closed my eyes for a second and took a deep breath. I could almost smell the burning flesh already. My arms and legs trembled the way they had when Zofia used to get angry with me. Only now, it wasn't because I was afraid.

It was because I was excited.

# Chapter 15

The aloe plant in the kitchen window had prickly leaves that tapered off at their ends. Mom kept it there in case she burned herself cooking. She'd probably gotten the idea from one of her health magazines.

I'd broken off a leaf, and now that I was back in my room, I used my Swiss Army knife to slit it open. Sticky clear-coloured juice dribbled out, and very gently, I applied some to my wrist. The hot spoon had left a scarlet welt that had already begun to blister along the edges.

I examined the burn, holding my arm at a distance so I could get a better look. My whole arm — no, my whole body — felt weak from the pain. I settled back on my pillows, careful to keep my wrist far away from the sheets. Right now, even the slightest touch would be unbearable.

At least this time there was no blood to worry

about. No Kleenex to flush down the toilet. My body was tired, but my mind was wide awake. Why in the world, I wondered now, had I gone and burned myself? Bad enough I sometimes cut myself, but this time, cutting hadn't been enough. I'd burned myself, too. What was wrong with me?

I'd wondered before if I was crazy — psycho — but now the idea seemed less weird.

What if I was *really* crazy? The kind of crazy person they lock up and put away? What if I could never stop hurting myself? And what if I ended up killing myself? *No*, I told myself, I *wasn't that bad*. If I really wanted to kill myself, I'd have done it by now. I'd have cut along the veins on my wrist, not across them. That way I'd have bled to death.

No, it wasn't death I wanted; it was pain. For some reason I didn't fully understand, I needed to feel pain. Over and over again.

I lifted my knees to my forehead and rocked back and forth on the small of my back. The movement comforted me, but at the same time, I couldn't help thinking how if anyone saw me right then, rocking on my bed, my wrist — cut and now burned — extended into the air, they'd definitely think I was nuts.

I'd never told anyone about the cutting. And unlike drugs and STDs, cutting wasn't a topic that ever came up in our moral and religious education classes at school. Maybe our teachers figured that talking about it would plant the idea in kids' minds.

Did anyone else I know cut themselves? My mind settled on the jeweller I'd met at Phillips Square — the woman with the scarred wrists. Her scars were pale and faded. She must have found a way to stop cutting. But what was it?

Thinking about her gave me courage. I had to learn more about cutting. If I understood it better, maybe then I'd be able to stop.

There had to be information on the Net. You could look up *anything* on the Net these days. Mom checked other real estate agents' listings; Dad checked his investments and the baseball stats, and Errol, well, who knows what Errol googled in his spare time?

I got up from my bed and turned on the computer. I hadn't used it since school ended. I'd been too busy with skating and well … other stuff.

At first, I wasn't sure what word to google. What did people call what I did? So I tried the words "people who hurt themselves." The first item was about some performance artist who locked himself in a two-by-three-foot locker for five days straight. Just thinking about it made me feel claustrophobic. After that, the artist — his name was Chris — made one of his friends shoot him in the arm.

I couldn't exactly relate.

I scanned the other matches. Self-sabotage. Sex injuries. Suicide attempts. No, none of that clicked for me, either. Then my eyes landed on the word "cutting." Simple and obvious. Why hadn't

I checked that first? So I went back and googled "cutting."

I felt a little dizzy when I got 348 million — MILLION! — matches. I clicked on something called "testimonials." A headshot of a girl my age popped up on the screen. Except for a really bad haircut — it looked like someone had put a bowl over her head and cut around it — she looked normal.

"My name is Alysyn," I read. "I've been in therapy for five years, but I can't stop cutting." I felt a pit in my stomach.

I clicked on another site about the history of cutting. There was a quote from the bible in bold print on the top of the page: "If your right eye is your trouble, gouge it out." I winced. At least, I'd never felt an urge to gouge out my eye. Or ask a friend to shoot me in the arm.

Then I read about how Oedipus — this guy in an old Greek play — had plucked out his eyes, and how nuns and saints in the middle ages believed that whipping themselves was a way to express their faith in God. Well, I'd never wanted to whip myself either. These people had it way worse than me.

The next site was the grossest. Some guy named Tony — apparently it wasn't just girls who cut themselves — had made a drawing, only he'd used blood instead of ink or paint. And Tony was so proud of his creation, he'd posted it on the Web for other sickos to enjoy. I couldn't get the mouse over quickly enough to hit the exit icon.

The next site, called "self-injury," was divided into two sections: "Why people injure themselves," and "Ways to stop self-injury." I went to the ways to stop first. "Self-injury," I read, "is sometimes used as a way to manage difficult feelings. Those wishing to reduce or stop self-injury must find healthier substitute behaviours to manage these difficult feelings." My eyes raced down the page to the list of suggested substitute behaviours the site recommended.

I snickered when I read the first one: "Go for a walk." As if something as simple as going for a walk could stop me from cutting — or burning — myself! Some of the other suggestions were plain stupid. "Use red wash-out hair colouring in the shower." Now how could that help?

When I got to the last suggestion — "Masturbate" — I felt my face get hot. Imagine telling someone to masturbate! I'd done it a few times, but it wasn't something I wanted to think about. Besides, what did it have to do with cutting? And how did I know this wasn't some porn site, anyway?

I switched over to the section on why people injure themselves. The page was full of tiny dark print. At least there were no lists of perverted suggestions. I began at the top: "There is a strong correlation between self-injury and childhood abuse. Individuals who have been subjected to emotional and/or physical pain in childhood sometimes seek to replicate that pain. What many of them report looking for is a sense of numbness — a similar numbness to the one experienced when they were undergoing the earlier abuse."

I sucked in my breath. *Oh my God,* I thought. *That's me.*

# Chapter 16

When the front door slammed, I knew it was Errol.

"Becks, you home?" he called out. "Mom and Dad gave me money for takeout, so I got some Indian food on the way home. Butter chicken, your fave. What'd you do — make popcorn? It smells like popcorn in here. Any left for your big bro?"

I felt my face get hot. I hadn't made popcorn. Could Errol be smelling burned flesh? I'd smelled it, too, at first, but then I thought the smell had gone away. Maybe I'd just stopped noticing it. Why hadn't I turned on the fan over the stove?

There was no point ignoring Errol. Usually, he either treated me like I was invisible or tried to annoy me, but there were other times — and this seemed to be one — when he actually wanted to talk. And I wasn't in a talking mood.

I opened my door a crack. "I'm not hungry. But don't eat all the butter chicken. Maybe I'll have some later." Then I shut my door. Hopefully, he'd get the message that I wanted to be left alone.

"What about that popcorn?"

This time, I didn't open my door.

"I didn't make any popcorn," I shouted.

For a couple of minutes, I thought I was safe — that Errol would leave me alone. I could imagine him heating up dinner in the microwave, then sitting down to eat at the dining room table. Considering how he felt about the rest of us, he probably preferred eating by himself.

But then I heard him rushing up the stairs. He was talking again, only I couldn't tell if it was to himself, or me. I heard him open his bedroom door and drop something on the bed.

"You should see this bullfrog helicopter I bought myself this afternoon. It's got bubble windows," he was saying.

Did he really think I cared?

I heard him pass my door. "Sure about that butter chicken?" he called out.

"I'm sure. I'm gonna lie down for a bit."

I could feel him standing outside my door. Why wouldn't he leave me alone?

"Ya know, Becky," he said at last. "I've been wondering … why'd you do it?"

For a split second, I wondered if Errol knew I'd burned myself. But no, there was no way he could have figured that out.

"Why'd you stop competing?"

I sucked in my breath. So that's what he was talking about. "Go away," I said sharply.

And he left.

***

I closed my eyes and thought back — way back — to the last time I'd competed.

It was the provincials and I was at the Eugène-Lalonde Arena in Sherbrooke, Quebec. I'd driven up from Montreal with my parents and Errol. Zofia had come in her own car.

There'd been a huge snowstorm the night before: thirty-two centimetres of snow had come down and the roads were treacherous. The drive, which usually takes about two hours, took more than three.

In the car, my parents had hardly said a word. Dad's eyes were glued to the snow-covered highway in front of him. Mom was perched like a bird on the edge of her seat, on the lookout for black ice.

I remember wishing I could find the words to tell them about my feet — how they were covered in painful blisters, how Band-Aids and Neosporin weren't helping anymore, and how even pulling on my sports socks made my eyes water. But I couldn't tell them. If I did, they'd get angry and blame me.

If there was one thing my parents agreed on, it

was that Zofia Lupescu was the best thing that had ever happened to us.

"Imagine our daughter being coached by a former Olympic athlete. I mean, what are the chances, Gwennie?" I'd heard my dad say to Mom when Zofia had first agreed to take me on as a private student.

"Becky is a very lucky girl," Mom had told him. "Zofia is tough, but that's what Becks needs if she's going to make it."

I was some lucky girl, all right.

Errol hadn't been too happy about waking up early. We were supposed to get up at 5:30 and leave the house at six, but Dad had woken us up at 4:30 instead. "There's been a blizzard and we need to get an earlier start," he'd whispered into my ear.

When he went into Errol's room, I could hear Errol moaning from across the hall. "Why do I have to go to her dumb competition anyway?"

My dad lowered his voice, but I could still hear him. "You have a responsibility to your sister. Besides," he said, "we're all very proud of her. Your sister is going places."

What he'd meant was that Errol was going nowhere. No wonder Errol hated me.

In the car, Errol snored as loudly as the snow blowers outside. His eyes were half-open, so I knew he wasn't really sleeping. The fake snoring was just another way to bug me.

My nerves were already shot because of the

competition, and when I couldn't take his snoring anymore, I kicked him. As hard as I could.

"Becky kicked me!" he shouted, proving he hadn't been asleep.

My mother turned to face us, momentarily distracted from black-ice patrol.

"Becky! Leave your brother alone. Think how nice he's being, coming along to see you compete today."

"He didn't want to come," I muttered.

"Of course I did," Errol said in a sugary voice that was even worse than the fake snoring.

I turned to look out the car window. The trees looked as if they were wearing white coats. Just then, Errol kicked me in the shin — way harder than I'd kicked him.

Only I didn't say anything about it. I was getting used to not complaining when somebody hurt me. That was something else I'd learned from my Olympic calibre coach.

*** 

The stands were so crowded, I couldn't see my parents or Errol — only the stony faces of the judges, seated together in the front row.

"Remember every-zing I taught you," Zofia told me when it was my turn to compete in the freestyle competition. We'd been working on my routine for nine months: apart from the usual artistic moves, I was going to do three double jumps and two spins. It was an ambitious program, even for me.

But just as I was skating out onto the ice, my legs beginning to feel like jelly, the way they always did before a competition, the arena went black. I was afraid, but at the same time, relieved. The soles of my feet were raw.

I heard whispers all around me, quickly growing louder. Someone flicked a lighter in the stands and for a moment, I could see an orange yellow flame. But then it was gone.

I couldn't see Zofia, but I could feel her next to me — her rough, impatient movements. She took hold of my upper arm. I tried to shake her hand loose, but she wouldn't release her grip. "Power failure," was all she said as she led me back to the stands.

Somehow, even in the pitch dark, my parents found their way over to where I was sitting.

"Bad timing," my dad said, patting my shoulder.

"I'm afraid Becky will lose her focus," my mom said, talking about me as if I wasn't there.

"Where's Errol?" I asked.

"Having a little nap. Mom said. "I'm surprised he's so tired, considering he slept the whole way over here this morning."

Yeah sure, I thought.

\*\*\*

Mom was right about one thing: I *was* losing my focus. Especially after the lights went on, flickered for a few seconds, and then went out again two more times before the electricity finally came back on for good. It wasn't just the rink that was affected by the power shortage; it was the entire city of Sherbrooke.

Once I skated out to the centre of the rink, the instrumentals from *The Last of the Mohicans* began drifting out of the loudspeakers. I kept my movements fluid, extending one arm in the air so my fingers were very long, just like Zofia had taught me. Then I circled my arm slowly, keeping time with the music. When the pain from my feet got more intense, I bit down on my lip.

The drumming started out slowly at first. That was my cue to prepare for my first double. Keeping my back straight, I tried to imagine myself doing the perfect double jump. One that even Zofia couldn't criticize.

But somehow, my mind wouldn't let me imagine a double jump. Only a single.

I felt a sick feeling in the pit of my stomach. Zofia would never forgive me if I screwed up. She'd be so angry, she might even drop me as a student. And then where would I be?

*Double jump*, I told myself as I leapt up into the air. Two rotations, one immediately following the other.

I completed the first rotation, my hands clasped in front of my chest, and my legs held tightly together. But then, instead of keeping everything tight and moving into the second rotation, I popped open, slowing down and losing momentum. I'd only done a single jump. A huge, high jump, but a single one — and of course, the judges would have noticed my mistake.

I kept my eyes straight ahead, staring at the scoreboard. There was one place I definitely wasn't going to look — at Zofia. My knees shook when I imagined how angry she was going to be.

After the single jump, I moved right into a spin. I felt myself relax a little as I spun. Then there were more artistic moves — all based on the choreography Zofia had designed for me.

When it was time for the second double jump, I did it, perfectly. Inside my head, I heard clapping. Was it the audience — or was I imagining it?

Now the second spin. I'd always loved spins. I straightened my head and spine. My back was as straight as the snow-covered fir trees I'd seen from the car window that morning.

A little more footwork, and then it was time for my final double jump. I didn't dare picture this one in my head — what if I screwed it up, the way I'd done with the first one?

I had to place in the provincials if I wanted to keep competing. And if I wanted to keep training with Zofia.

That's when I fell. Flat on my bottom, as if I was just learning to skate.

The audience groaned.

I could imagine my mother holding her hand in front of her mouth, Dad's arm around her waist as he tried to comfort her. I could imagine Errol's smirk and Zofia's flashing eyes.

I went through the motions of the final artistic movements, the ones that led me off the ice. I did them without making any mistakes, but without heart. Like an ice princess. A useless bitch. Ice princesses and useless bitches didn't place at the provincials. Champion figure skaters skated with heart.

One thing for sure: my figure skating career was over.

I felt sad and a little ashamed — everyone had seen me screw up — but I felt something else, too. A feeling that took me by surprise. Relief.

Zofia was waiting at the boards, her arms crossed over her chest, when I got off the ice. "What were you thinking, you bitch?" she cried out as I stepped off the ice. "You useless bitch!"

I hunched my shoulders, wishing I could disappear. But then Zofia grabbed my arm and began leading me towards the hallway that led to the locker room. I knew if I resisted, she'd only pull harder.

Just then, someone else appeared, a man I didn't recognize. He must've been another coach. "Calm down, Madame Lupescu!" he said, pulling her off me and back towards the stands.

I could feel other skaters watching, pitying me.

But their eyes didn't stay on me for long. Maybe they were worried what had happened to me could happen to them. That they might screw up, too.

Zofia was shouting again.

"How could you be zuch an idiot?"

I blocked my ears to make the sound of her voice go away. But that was silly. I'd only been remembering her voice.

A word I'd seen before on the computer screen suddenly flashed in my head: "self-sabotage." That was it: I'd sabotaged myself. Destroyed my career as a competitive skater.

That was why I'd done it.

At least Zofia Lupescu was out of my life. Or at least, I hoped she was.

# Chapter 17

"Know what you said about our final show, Miss Becky? Well, um … I don't think I'm good enough."

"Of course you're good enough," I told Tara as I kneeled down to help her take off her skates. "Besides, like I explained on the ice before — every girl performs at her own level. Plus, you get to choose your own music. That's part of what makes the show so much fun."

I really had to work to get Tara's skates off.

"You know, young lady," I told her as I tugged, "it could be time for a bigger pair of skates."

"Uh-oh," Tara said, chewing on the inside of her cheek. "My mom got me these skates when camp started. I wanted snowflakes," she said, pointing at a blue snowflake design on the tongue of one of her skates.

I lifted Tara's foot into the air and inspected her

heel. The blood had run through her heavy sock.

"Uh-oh," I said, wincing. "A blister. Those can be real painful. Let's get you a Band-Aid straightaway. You know, you're going to be a much better skater when you're wearing skates that fit you right."

"I will?" Tara seemed to have forgotten about the snowflake design. But then her face got serious again. "My mom won't want to spend more money on skates. She told me my feet better not grow till next year."

Amy was sitting next to Tara on the bench.

"Of course she'll buy you new skates. She won't want you getting blisters."

Tara's eyes dropped to the locker room floor.

I peered inside one of her skates. "Size three," I said. "You know, I think I just might have a pair of size three and a half, from when I was your age. They're in some old crate in our basement. I'm going to find them for you. How's that sound?"

Tara squeezed my hand. "*Your* old skates?" From the way she said it, you'd think they were a collector's item.

"They aren't just any old skates," I said as I squeezed back. "They're my old *lucky* skates. The ones I wore when I first started competing."

Amy was drying her blades with a rag.

"So did you meet Zofia yet?" I tried to keep my voice casual, but it quivered when I said Zofia's name.

"Not yet. But she's coming here to give me a trial lesson."

I don't know why I was so surprised. Of course, Zofia would want to audition a new skater to see whether she was worth taking on. But I'd thought Zofia would insist that Amy come to the rink where Zofia usually worked.

"When's the lesson?" This time, there was no question about it. My voice squeaked like an old rusty hinge.

"Friday, I think."

I sucked in my breath. Zofia was coming here. In two days. "Your mom picking you up today?" I asked Amy.

"Nah, my babysitter's coming. My mom's got an appointment — at the hairdresser." I thought of Mrs. Gross's perfectly coiffed hair.

Amy twirled her bracelet. It was the one I'd given her.

"How come you didn't get yourself a bracelet too, Miss Becky?" Tara asked when she saw me looking at Amy's.

"I don't like the way bracelets feel against my wrist."

Though I'd been trying to avoid the question, it pleased me that my answer was so close to the truth.

\*\*\*

Tory was waiting for me outside the rec centre when camp ended for the day.

"Hey, what you up to?" he asked.

I quickened my pace. "Nothing much."

"What I mean is," Tory continued — he was walking beside me now — "do you want to do something?" He sounded like he was out of breath, which seemed kind of strange for a hockey player.

I turned to face him. "I was gonna go for a walk."

I don't why I said that. I'd been planning to go home and look for that pair of skates I'd promised Tara.

"Mind if I join you?"

I smiled at Tory. It was the first time I'd noticed there were freckles on the tip of his nose. "Why should I mind?"

"Where exactly are we going?" Tory asked after we'd been walking in silence for about ten minutes.

"Downtown," I told him. "Near Phillip's Square."

"Downtown? Are you nuts, Becky? That'll take us, like, another hour. Maybe more."

"It's good exercise."

"Don't you get enough exercise on the ice?"

"You don't have to come."

But Tory kept walking next to me. There was something nice about seeing our two pairs of sneakers keeping pace along the sidewalk. Still, I was happier when he wasn't trying to make conversation.

In the end, I was the one who started talking. By

then, we were at the Polish bakery near the corner of Sherbrooke Street, and Decarie Boulevard. The sweet smell of donuts competed with car fumes. Because we were so close to the highway, I had to raise my voice.

"It looks like one of the girls in my group might be training with Zofia."

Tory groaned. "You're kidding."

Once we'd crossed Decarie, he led me to a bench in front of a grey stone church. "Y'know, ever since you told me about Zofia and how she treated you, I started remembering stuff, too." There were tiny lines on Tory's forehead. "I once saw her pull you off the ice. And you weren't the only one she gave a hard time to. She yelled like crazy at other girls, too. She made a couple of them cry. That woman shouldn't be allowed to work with kids."

Tory looked up at me. "So what are you going to do to help that girl in your group?"

"I'm still trying to figure that one out."

Tory nodded. For a moment, his hand brushed against mine. I could have moved closer to him, but I didn't.

***

"Wanna go for a cold drink — or an ice cream?" Tory asked when we were nearly at Phillip's Square. His cheeks were covered with tiny droplets of sweat. "*Sweat is the body's natural cooling system*," I imagined my mom's voice saying. Of course if it was me sweating, she'd add something about how if a person slimmed down, she might sweat less. And it wouldn't take Albert Einstein to know that person was me.

My eyes scanned the little park across from the Bay. The vendors were out, but I couldn't see who I was looking for. Maybe she'd gone home for the day — or maybe someone else was minding her booth.

"We could go to that coffee shop," I said, pointing to a Van Houtte facing Phillip's Square. If we got a seat by the window, I could watch for my … "friend" wasn't exactly the right word.

"Why'd you stop competing?" Tory asked once we'd ordered two ice coffees and brought them over to our table.

"Too much pressure," I said. "Plus, I was putting on weight." I squirmed a little in my seat. This wasn't exactly my favourite topic.

Tory nodded, which made me wonder if he thought I was fat.

"Was it because of Zofia?"

When I lifted my glass, the ice make a clinking sound.

"Here's a toast to Zofia Lupescu," I said, "who made me what I am today."

Tory didn't lift his glass from the table.

I suddenly remembered how, when I'd get home after those days Zofia coached me, I'd head right for the kitchen, to pig out on cookies and ice cream bars. I was hungry, but it was more than that. I must have known that if I got too heavy, I wouldn't be able to keep competing. Eating became a way out. Another kind of self-sabotage.

"What about you?" I asked Tory. "Why didn't you keep playing hockey, competitively, I mean?"

This time, Tory raised his glass to mine. "I wasn't good enough." From the way he smiled, I was pretty sure he was over it. Or mostly over it.

"So it's not so bad, is it — spending time with me?" Tory looked at me over the frothy top of his ice coffee.

"No, it's not."

\*\*\*

The bathroom was all the way at the back of the café. I glanced at my reflection in the mirror as I washed my hands. I smiled — just to see how my face looked when I smiled. Not bad. A little chubby, but okay. Not Miss Perfect the way Errol imagined, but almost normal … that is, if you didn't know too much about me.

I hardly noticed when someone else walked out of the other stall and joined me at the row of sinks. I recognized her long, suntanned fingers. An artist's hands. A faint smell of patchouli filled the air.

She must have recognized me, too, because she smiled. Her front teeth looked grey.

"Bonjour," she said. "You're the girl who

bought so many of my bracelets — for your skaters."

I felt myself blush. "They really like the bracelets. They wear them every day."

"That's good. Thank you for telling me. Merci."

When she reached for my arm, I took a step back. My spine nearly touched the tile wall. For a second, the light caught her wrist and I saw them again — the pale scars, running like tracks across her veins.

I knew she could tell I'd seen them.

"How did you stop?" I asked her.

She looked right at me. Her eyes seemed very sad, as if she'd gone someplace far away. "One day I just stopped. But it went on for years. Too long. Don't let it go on that long for you."

She stepped towards the door.

"There's one more thing," I said. "Did anyone ever, you know, hurt you when you were growing up?"

When her body stiffened, I knew the answer.

# Chapter 18

The basement was piled high with cardboard boxes, all labeled in Mom's neat handwriting. It was all either stuff we didn't use, or had never unpacked after our last move. "Soup tureen and matching ladle." "Punch bowl set." "Becky — baby clothes." Which meant I was getting warmer.

"What are you doing down there, making such a racket?" Mom called out from the dining room. "I'm working on my accounts."

I got out from behind a pile of boxes and walked closer to the basement door so I wouldn't have to shout. "I'm looking for a pair of old skates."

"Whatever for?" Mom sounded irritated, but I figured it had more to do with her accounts than me. She always got into a bad mood when she had to do paperwork.

"I want to give them to this girl at skating — Tara."

My mother made an exasperated groan, so loud I could hear it downstairs. "Why can't she get her own skates?"

I didn't feel like explaining. Besides, I got the feeling my mom didn't really want to know. So I went back to looking. "Errol — baby clothes." Nope. "Hallowe'en costumes." Nope.

There were more boxes in the crawl space under the stairway. I had to crouch to reach them. The top box was covered with a thick layer of dust that rose into the air like a cloud when I blew on it. Which made me sneeze.

"Becks? Are you catching a cold?" my mom called out.

"I'm fine. Aren't you supposed to be doing your accounts?"

"Skates — Rebecca." I'd hit pay dirt. I tore open the box, which was taped shut with a thick strip of packing tape. When I opened it, I smelled mildew and leather, and a dry smell that reminded me of sawdust.

There were four pairs of skates inside the box, their blades carefully wrapped in shredded newspaper. Leave it to my mom to worry about someone cutting themselves. *If she only knew,* I thought, as I glanced at my wrist. With all the reaching and tearing I'd been doing, my long sleeves had begun to inch up my arms. Out of habit, I pulled them down. The burn mark from the spoon had turned pink.

Mom had arranged the skates according to size.

I smiled when I unwrapped the first pair. Had my feet really been that small?

I crossed my legs so I'd be more comfortable. I could feel more memories coming back as I lay the skates in my lap. Skating with my dad — just the two of us — on the outdoor rink at the end of the street we'd lived on. My dad's skates were made of brown leather. He'd skated backwards so he could catch me if I fell.

I could still hear the tinkling sound of his laughter as he joked with the other dads, and how red his cheeks had looked.

In the end, he'd been the one to fall, not me. And he'd broken his glasses. Cracked the lenses on both sides. And then I remembered helping him off the ice. He couldn't see without his glasses. Someone else's dad had to drive us home.

The next pair of skates had that blue snowflake logo on the tongues — the same snowflake that was on Tara's pair of too-small skates. How silly to put up with blisters just for some snowflake! But when I looked at the snowflake again, I could see why she liked it: it was bright blue, the colour of a cornflower, and it was perfectly symmetrical, tiny triangles layered over other tiny triangles.

But I couldn't remember paying much attention to the snowflakes when I'd worn those skates. Was it because, by then, I was already starting to take skating more seriously? Was it because, by then, I'd shown a talent for skating — and because group lessons weren't doing enough for me, my parents had started looking for a private coach for me to work with?

And now Amy was in the very same situation.

I felt my body flinch. It was stronger than a shiver — more like an electric shock that ran up my spine and made my shoulders creep up towards my neck.

Zofia.

I wasn't afraid for myself. I was afraid for Amy.

I had to do something.

When I unwrapped the next pair of skates — size three and a half Riddells — I was even more convinced I had to do something. That's because when I ran the old frayed laces between my fingers, I noticed they weren't just yellow with age, they were flecked with rust.

Only I knew it wasn't rust.

It was blood. And when I started to unlace one of the skates, something popped out.

At first, I was confused. How did one of Errol's old Lego blocks find its way here? But as it tumbled onto the floor, it didn't make the hollow clattering sound I expected. That's because it was rubber. Hard rubber. One of the arch supports Zofia had made me wear to fix my flat feet. I pushed the skate aside and let the rubber arch support lie on the floor.

I pulled off the gym socks I was wearing and turned over my feet so I could see my soles. I ran my fingers along the skin near the middle of my foot.

The skin felt rough.

More scars. I'd never noticed them before.

I waited a while before I went upstairs.

"Did you find them?" my mom called out. She sounded less stressed than before.

"Uh-huh."

"You know," she said, and I was glad she didn't get up from the dining room table. "I don't tell you this often enough, but you're a good person, Becks. A generous person."

I kept walking. I didn't want her to know I was upset. And if I said thanks to her now, I thought I might cry.

The first thing I did when I got to my room was look over at my pencil tin.

I could tell right away that someone had moved it ever so slightly. It wasn't lined up with my blotter the way it always was. I rushed over to my desk and already I could feel a cool sweat building under my armpits and behind my knees.

My Swiss Army knife was gone.

# Chapter 19

Errol's door was closed, but I knew he was in there. I could tell from the stripe of light under the door — and from the plastic cement fumes. I pounded on the door with my fist.

"Errol!" I shouted. "Were you in my room?"

I pounded so hard the door flew open. Errol was sitting on the wood floor, crouched over his latest model — that helicopter with the fancy windows. For a second, I wondered if my brother's obsession with planes was a sign he wished he could escape — fly away from our dysfunctional family.

Errol was using a toothpick to remove leftover plastic cement from one of the helicopter's wings.

"Who's in whose room?" he asked in a bored voice, without looking up at me.

"You heard me!" I could feel the blood rushing to my head. It *had* to be him! And he knew better than to go poking around in my private stuff. Imagine if I went messing with his dumb models.

"Were you in my room?" I asked again. I scanned the floor and the top of his bureau and desk for my Swiss Army knife. No sign of it.

"Why would I want to go into *your* room?"

A chair scraped against the floor downstairs.

"Darling, dear, are the two of you having a problem?" Mom called out in a forced, cheerful voice. She hated when Errol and I got into a fight.

"No. Everything's fine," Errol called back. He sounded as cheerful as Mom. Talk about messed-up.

I lowered my voice. "Give it back," I hissed. "Right now."

Errol lifted the helicopter from the floor and circled it in the air. "Zoom, zoom!" he said. You'd think he was seven years old. I knew he'd made the zooming noises just to bug me, so I tried to ignore him.

"D'you like my helicopter?" he asked as the circles he was making got smaller and closer to his body. At least now he was looking at me.

"It's fine," I said, swallowing hard. "It's very nice. But give it back to me."

Errol made the helicopter hover a few inches over the floor. "Give *what* back to you?"

When he said that, I knew for sure he had my knife.

"I want it back."

Our eyes met. I wanted Errol to know I was

serious. For a split second, I imagined grabbing his helicopter and stepping on it — sending all the little bits he'd cemented so carefully together flying in every direction.

"If I wanted to, I could …" I said, letting my voice trail off. I knew I'd never do it.

"Give *what* back to you?" Errol said, taunting me.

Then just like that, my anger started seeping out of me and I felt my eyes fill with tears. How could Errol be so mean?

"My knife," I whispered, blinking to make the tears go away.

Errol put the helicopter down on the floor. "No way," he said.

I didn't know what to do next. I needed my knife. Not to cut myself. Just to have it. In case.

Knowing the knife was in my pencil tin gave me a strange kind of security. But that didn't make any sense. How could something I used to hurt myself make me feel secure? My head was starting to ache from the angry and sad feelings I was holding inside.

The knife would make me feel better. Just having it, knowing it was there.

But Errol wouldn't give it back. I shuddered when I imagined him opening it up and finding the dried droplets of blood on the blade. How could he? He'd ignored my privacy as much as if he'd read my journal or gone through my underwear drawer.

"I need it," I said, just managing to get the words out. "I need my knife."

Errol put the helicopter down on his desk. When he spoke, his voice was different, more serious.

"I'm on to you, Becky. It took me a while, but I finally figured out why you spend so much time locked up in your room. At first, it was just a feeling, but then I went looking in your room."

"How dare you!" I was getting angry all over again.

"Don't you see Becky — that's not the point? I may be an asshole, but I won't let you do it anymore. It's sick."

"You can't stop me!"

I wanted to slam Errol's door, but I definitely didn't want Mom knowing what was going on. So I closed it instead. At least I wouldn't have to see his dumb face, or listen to him calling me "sick."

For a few seconds, I just stood in the hallway outside his room. He could have apologized for going through my stuff, or given me back my knife. But all he did was turn on his techno music.

*I hate you*, I thought. *Do I ever hate you!*

Now what was I supposed to do? I felt like a trapped animal. There was no place for me to go. No place to escape to.

*Making something helps.* The words popped into my head. But I was way too upset to draw.

No, I knew what I'd do. I'd go into the kitchen and turn up the heat on the front burner. I bit my lip as I imagined pressing my wrist down on the hot flame. I could almost imagine the pain, and the flood of relief that would come with it.

But then another part of me took over: *Are you nuts?* it asked. *And what about Mom? Don't you think she'd notice you cooking yourself on her fancy-ass gas stove, not to mention the smell of burnt flesh?*

*Becky Sanger*, that other part of me said, *you're going too far. Way too far. You're spiraling out of control. You've got to do something.*

But what?

I headed downstairs to the kitchen. Mom was organizing papers at the dining room table.

"It sounds like you and your brother straightened things out. I'm going to make myself a cup of green tea. Would you like one, darling? It's full of antioxidants." I tried not to laugh. Right then, I needed way more than antioxidants.

I opened the pantry. "Nah," I said as I checked the shelves for the thin packet I was looking for. I hadn't had Kool-Aid in years, but because Errol liked it, Mom usually kept some in the house — despite her feelings about food colouring and artificial sweetener.

It was the food colouring I was after.

I found it — Errol's favourite: cherry-flavoured. It was behind the all-natural cashew butter. It would have to do instead of wash-out hair colour.

"What are you doing in the pantry, Becks?"

"Just looking for something to eat."

"There's carrot sticks in the fridge."

Of course there were.

\*\*\*

It was only when I was standing under the shower, the red tinted water streaming over my naked body, and then onto the bathtub floor, that I got the point.

It was like blood. Thinner, of course, and way brighter, less metallic. But still, a decent substitute. I took several deep breaths and tried to concentrate on the colour red.

I watched the droplets pool around my feet and then make their way down the drain in a current of red.

The warm air was heavy with the sweet smell of Kool-Aid. I licked my lips. Gross. Way too sweet.

But the weird thing was: I started feeling a little calmer. Just a little.

Maybe, for now, it was all I could ask for.

## Chapter 20

I nearly lost my breath when I saw her. Big black wavy hair, big black eyes made even darker by the thick layers of mascara globbed on her lashes. Zofia hadn't changed much since I'd last seen her — about four years ago, when I gave up competitive skating. But, somehow, it was her tone of voice that upset me most.

"Start by showing me your spins," I heard her tell Amy. "Scratch foot spin first." The words came out sharply and without much rhythm, sounding more like an order than a request. I knew how much Zofia liked giving orders.

Amy smiled and did exactly what she was told. Poor kid had no idea what she was in for.

Unless I did something about it.

Amy had no trouble with the scratch foot spin. We'd been working on her spins and jumps at lunchtime, and by now, she could do a scratch foot blindfolded, if she had to. She spun round like a top, her palms pressed together over her head. Lovely.

Zofia nodded. I guess that meant she still didn't believe in compliments. "Camel spin next," she barked as she stopped to jot something down on her clipboard.

I spotted Mrs. Gross watching from the sideboards, her hair perfectly in place and smiling like the Virgin Mary in some old religious painting. It was all about her, of course. If Amy became a prize-winning skater, and at such a young age, too, that would make Mrs. Gross a prize-winning mother. Her blue eyes were glazed over, already picturing the medals and trophies, maybe even the Olympic medal in her — I should say her daughter's — future. I'd seen that same look in my mom's eyes.

All Zofia did was nod when I walked over to join Mrs. Gross. A short, curt nod, no different from the one she'd given Amy after her scratch foot spin. Waving would have taken too much energy — and Zofia had made it clear long ago I wasn't worth the energy she'd put into me.

"*Useless bitch!*" The words rang in my ears, distracting me as I tried to concentrate on Amy's camel spin. Amy leaned forward, raising one leg up behind her, and began to spin. When she was done, her cheeks were red and her brown eyes were shining.

"How did I do?" she asked Zofia in a breathless voice.

When Zofia nodded, I saw what looked like a shadow cross Amy's face. I knew exactly what she was thinking: Had she done something wrong? Had she somehow disappointed Zofia? And what could she do to win Zofia's approval? That was the way I'd felt when Zofia was my coach. I'd have done just about anything to get her approval.

Thank God Amy didn't have flat feet. The thought made the old pain in my arches kick in — a dull throb that slowly got sharper. My body was remembering again.

Zofia wanted Amy to do a sit spin next, only she pronounced it "zit spin." Amy shifted on the ice and caught my eye. I could tell she wanted to know if I'd heard Zofia say "zit." I liked that Amy noticed Zofia's accent. It meant she knew Zofia wasn't perfect, and hopefully, it would help her stand up to Zofia when the time came. If the time came.

When I grinned, Amy grinned back — a toothy smile that reminded me she was just a kid. A helpless, eager-to-please, talented kid. Not much different from the kid I'd been.

Automatically, I checked to see whether Zofia had noticed. She'd be angry if she caught us laughing at her — and you didn't want to do anything to make Zofia angry.

That's when I caught myself. *What do you care if you make Zofia angry?* I asked myself. *She can't do anything to you — not anymore. Why does she still have a hold over you — even after all these years?*

Amy's body hovered just an inch or two over the ice as she did her sit spin.

"She's really good," I whispered under my breath.

Mrs. Gross beamed with satisfaction. "I know," she whispered back, without taking her eyes off of Amy.

"Another zit spin!" Zofia called out. It was one of the hardest spins, and I knew she'd asked for another because she wanted to push Amy. Nothing was ever good enough for Zofia. If you did something well, she'd want to push you into doing it better. It was her strategy to improve kids' skating, but I knew it wasn't worth it. Not if it broke their spirits.

This time though, Amy didn't spin quickly enough. I felt a pit in my stomach as I pictured what was about to happen. Without enough speed to propel her, Amy would lose her footing. And just as I'd predicted, instead of hovering over the ice as she spun, Amy ended up spinning onto her bottom, her legs splayed out in front of her.

I clenched my fists as I watched for Zofia's reaction. When her dark eyes got even darker, I felt my whole body tense up.

"What's wrong?" Mrs. Gross said, turning to look at me.

It was hard to find the right words. "Zofia doesn't like mistakes," was all I managed to say.

Mrs. Gross smiled as she turned her eyes back to the ice.

"That's probably what makes her such a good coach," she said.

\*\*\*

I wasn't surprised when Zofia told Amy to take a break after she screwed up the "zit spin." Zofia probably needed a time out so she could go chew on her elbow or something.

Looking back, it probably wasn't the best time to talk to Zofia, but I figured it might be my only chance to get her alone. I didn't want anyone else to hear what I had to say.

"Zofia," I whispered as I walked over to the end of the rink, where she was writing notes on her clipboard. I needed to practice saying her name. I didn't want to get choked up when I talked to her. I didn't want her thinking that after all these years, she could still intimidate me.

As I got closer, I saw that Zofia had taken off her gloves. I could tell from the stiff way she was holding her fingers she was still upset. When she'd been my coach, I'd learned the signs — and there were lots — that she was upset: the stiff fingers, the flashing eyes, the throbbing vein on the side of her forehead.

"Zo — " I tried calling out, but it was as if I'd lost my voice.

My cheeks felt hot. There was still time to turn back. Zofia hadn't noticed me walking over towards her. Then I took another look at her fingers. This time, I remembered the bruises those fingers had left on my upper arm.

"Zofia!" This time, the sound came out. My voice didn't squeak, though it didn't sound quite right. It sounded too happy — almost as if I was glad to see her. Which I most definitely wasn't.

When Zofia looked up from her clipboard, I could feel her eyes on me. When her gaze lingered on my hips, I knew what she was thinking: that I was fat. I tried not to care. Right now, I had more important things on my mind.

"Becky. Becky Zanger," Zofia said, tapping the side of her face as if she'd had trouble remembering my name. She wanted me to know I didn't matter to her, that I never had.

That part didn't really bother me. What bothered me, I realized, when Zofia smiled a big phony smile and asked me how I was doing, was that she didn't feel guilty. Not even after everything she'd done to me.

I didn't bother answering her question. She didn't care how I was. She'd never cared. I forced myself to look into her black eyes — dark deep swampy pools, the kind you drown in. I fought the urge to turn away.

"You can't ..." I began, and then suddenly, I forgot what I was going to say. I just stood there, with my mouth hanging open. It was as if I was a little girl again, and Zofia was still my coach. For a second, I felt like I really was going to drown.

But then, I saw myself — standing there silently, feeling defeated. *You're not a helpless little girl anymore, Becky Sanger. You're fifteen and Zofia Lupescu can't hurt you anymore.*

"You can't coach Amy," I said. The tone of my voice surprised me. I sounded sure of myself, strong. A lot more confident than I really felt. It was easier for me to stand up for someone else than to stand up for myself.

When Zofia's eyes flashed, I felt a bit of my old nervousness came back. My mouth was dry and my stomach muscles clenched. But at least this time, my arms and legs didn't shake.

"Vat are you talking about?"

*Keep your balance,* I told myself. *Go ahead and say what you planned to say.*

"I won't let you do to Amy what you did to me." There, the words were out. Only instead of feeling proud or relieved, I felt this heaviness at the back of my throat. *Don't cry,* I told myself. *Don't let Zofia see she still has power over you.*

Zofia took a step in my direction.

When I took a step back, Zofia smiled. This time, it wasn't a fake smile. She knew I was still frightened of her — and she liked that.

"Whatever happened to you," she said, curling her lip in disgust as she eyed my hips, "you did to yourself. You had potential. But you wasted it."

When she said the word "wasted," it sounded as if she was spitting. "This girl, this Amy, she has potential, too."

Zofia hadn't even asked what she'd done to me. Clearly, in her mind, my failure to become a high-ranking competitive skater was my fault. I didn't care about my skating career anymore. I cared about what had happened to *me*. And I wanted Zofia to know it.

"The way you treated me …" I said, and now my voice was shaking for real, but I made myself go on anyway. I didn't care anymore if she saw me cry. "The names you called me, 'useless bitch,'" I said, in a voice that was so much like Zofia's that for a moment, I was startled. "The way you used to pinch my arm, those sick arch supports you made me wear that blistered my feet, the way you forced me to skate even with the blisters… the blood…"

The colour drained from Zofia's face, and when she spoke her voice was quieter.

"You had flat feet. You weren't strong enough," she said.

"No one would be strong enough."

Zofia made a snorting sound. "I have no time for you," she said, looking back down at her clipboard. It was clear I was dismissed.

I nearly turned away, but I didn't. I wasn't finished yet. This time, I was the one to step closer, and this time, Zofia backed away. And this time, I smiled.

The next few moments seemed to pass almost in slow motion. Zofia and I both stood completely still, watching each other. Let her think I

143

was fat and that I'd botched up my skating career. Zofia had gotten away with too much, for too long. I couldn't change the past, but now, when I finally had the chance, if I didn't stand up for Amy, I knew I'd always regret it. Yes, I wanted Zofia to understand what she'd done to me. But more than that, I needed to say the words out loud. For Amy and all the skaters that would come after her. And for me.

Slowly, keeping my eyes on Zofia's face the whole time, I rolled up my sleeve. It was the first time I'd ever shown anyone my scars.

I heard the soft sound of Zofia sucking in her breath. Then she whispered something in Romanian that sounded like a prayer.

"I did it because of you," I said.

When I looked at Zofia's face, I noticed the tiny lines around her eyes and over her upper lip.

"Don't say zat," Zofia whispered.

"You tell Mrs. Gross you can't take Amy on. Give her the name of another coach. One who isn't sick."

Zofia turned even paler, but when she spoke, her voice had returned to its usual volume. "Don't think you can tell me vat to do."

"You'll do it, or I'll tell everyone what happened to me." I said, "I'll *show them* too."

I couldn't say whether her eyes flashed, because by then, I'd turned my back and walked away.

This time, I really was shaking. My body felt

drained, as if I'd emptied myself out. I took a deep breath, letting the air fill not just my lungs, but my whole body. I'd done it. I hadn't been sure I could, but I'd done it.

# Chapter 21

Mom was at an open house. Dad had gone to play golf with my Uncle Bob. As for me, I was doing my best to ignore Errol.

I'd gone to a bookstore downtown and bought this book on self-injury. I'd waited till there was no one else at the cash register, so the only person I had to face was the clerk. But he hardly looked at the cover, and when he put the book in a bag, he yawned.

One of the reasons I picked it was that it was written by a psychology professor at Harvard, only she didn't use her real name. In the introduction, she made a point of saying how there's still a lot of shame attached to self-injury. She also says how self-injury is like what bulimia was ten years ago. It's pretty clear she thinks not talking about it is part of the problem. Which made me wonder why she didn't go ahead and use her real name on the cover.

I was just starting to read a chapter on how self-injury is like an addiction, when Errol knocked on my door.

"When did you learn to knock?" I asked as I tucked the book under my pillow and got up from my bed. "I thought you just barged into people's rooms and stole their stuff!"

When I opened the door, Errol had his hands in the pockets of his baggy jeans. I could tell he was uncomfortable.

"We should talk," he said.

"I don't see why." I tried closing the door on him, but Errol blocked it with his foot. I shrugged my shoulders.

"Okay, fine," I said, letting him in. Sometimes, dealing with Errol is like dealing with my mom: fighting just makes things worse. The sooner you give in, the sooner they go away and you can get on with other stuff.

Errol plopped himself down in the chair at my desk. Then he put his hands on his knees. I could tell he was getting into big brother mode.

"You know Becks, you should really talk to Dr. Sewell."

"Why? He hasn't done much to help you." It wasn't a nice thing to say, but I couldn't resist. Besides, Errol was the last person on earth I wanted advice from.

But Errol didn't seem annoyed. Instead, the corners of his lips lifted, like he was holding in a smile.

"How do you know he hasn't helped me?"

"Well, for one thing, you still spend every waking minute on your models or listening to techno. Let's just say you have no life, bro."

Errol brushed his hair out of his eyes. "I'm going back to school," he said in a quiet voice. "Not for anything academic. I signed up for this two-year cabinetmaking program."

"You did?" I was so surprised that for a moment, I forgot I was mad at him.

"Yeah, I did." Errol looked down at the floor. "You're actually the first one I'm telling."

"Cabinetmaking sounds great. Maybe it'll be like making models."

It felt weird to be having an ordinary conversation with Errol. I kept thinking he was about to tease me or say something stupid, but he didn't. And I could tell from the way Errol kept looking up at me, and then back down at the floor, that he was a little uncomfortable, too.

"Mom'll be in heaven when she hears about the cabinetmaking. Dad too."

"Yeah. Maybe she'll quit nagging you about your diet."

"Fat chance," I said, and we both laughed.

I knew I had to say something about my Swiss Army knife.

"You know, just because you took it away doesn't mean I'm going to stop." I paused for a second, considering whether I should go on. After all, I didn't know how much Errol knew.

But when I looked up at him, he was watching my face as intently as if I was some fighter jet he was working on. Errol knew.

"There's knives everywhere," I told him. "And hot stoves, too."

Errol didn't look shocked. Instead all he did was nod.

"That's why you should talk to Dr. Sewell."

"Did you tell him?" I asked, and I could feel the anger welling up in me again. If Errol had told, I'd never forgive him. Never.

"No way," Errol said. "I got my own troubles to deal with."

When Errol got up to leave, I followed him to the door.

"By the way," he said, turning to look back at me. "Who's that guy you're hanging out with?"

"What guy?"

"The one you met at the corner last night. Approximately 8:32 p.m."

"What do you do — spy on me when the parts are drying on your models?"

"I just happened to be looking out my window. Besides, I'm your brother. So who is he?"

"He's just a friend. From camp. We went out to see a movie."

"Just make sure he treats you right."

I didn't want to admit it at the time, but Errol had a point there. You had to make sure people treated you right. And if they didn't, you had to stand up and do something about it.

"Errol, you're a pain in the butt," I told him as I closed my door. "But I still think it's great about the cabinetmaking."

*** 

It's hard to get out of bed some Monday mornings.

But it wasn't that kind of Monday. I got to camp early. I'd been having these urges to skate round and round the rink, the way I used to when I first discovered I loved skating. Stroking like that had always been a good time for me to think — and I had a lot to think about: whether or not I wanted to talk to Dr. Sewell about the cutting; my feelings for Tory — for now we were just friends, but I was pretty sure he wanted more; and all the memories that had come back to me in the last few weeks.

The rink was dark, but it wasn't empty, like I'd expected. I could hear the sound of someone's blades cutting the ice. At first, I thought it might be Tory. When I'd gone skating early one morning the week before, he'd been out on the ice, too.

"May I?" he'd asked, then he'd reached for my hand, and we'd circled the rink together.

But it was Amy, not Tory.

"Hey!" I called out when I saw her. "What are you doing here so early?"

Amy skated over to me. "I came to practice. My new coach wants me to practice every morning before camp. So my dad dropped me off at 7:15 on his way —"

"That's great!" I said, trying to sound like I meant it. "When's your first session with..." I stopped to take a breath before I said her name, "...Zofia?"

Amy's lips tightened. *Oh no*, I thought, *Zofia is already stressing her out and they haven't even started working together.* So much for my Monday morning energy. I suddenly felt drained as I considered what was ahead for Amy — not just the long hours practising, but also the insults, and eventually, the abuse. I knew that even if Amy's feet weren't flat, Zofia would find some way to torture her. I was starting to understand that people like Zofia loved having power over others. Making them feel small made Zofia feel big and important. But maybe I could find some way to help Amy be strong so she could face Zofia and handle her better than I had.

"Zofia's too busy to have me as a student. She recommended another coach. This lady named Laura."

"Too busy?" For a second, I felt as if the ice was moving underneath me. She wasn't going to coach Amy! My standing up to Zofia really had made a difference!

Amy shifted from one skate to the other.

"Are you very disappointed?" I asked her. "I know your mom really wanted you to work with Zofia." For once, I didn't have trouble saying her name.

"At first I was," Amy said, looking up at me. "But I got over it."

"Just like that?" I patted Amy's shoulder.

Amy smiled up at me.

"Well, I tried to do what you said."

"What do you mean?"

"You know, what you said about picking yourself up when you fall. Well that's what I did. I picked myself up."

I joined Amy on the ice, and the two of us stroked around the rink, not saying anything at all. I thought how, in a way, because of everything that had happened to me, I'd fallen too. I'd fallen pretty hard and pretty low, into a kind of dark pit. But for the first time in a long while, I had the feeling that, like Amy, I just might be able to pick myself up.